## "I War[                ]
## I Don't Make [                ]
## Women Into My Arms Like That."

He ran a hand through his hair, looked around. Out the corner of her eye, she saw him crack a lame smile. "Must be something in the air."

She closed her eyes and withered. If she could turn back time and wipe out these past few moments, she'd do it in a blink. That she'd surrendered so completely was bad enough. Did he need to rub in the fact that he regretted it, too?

"Daniel, please don't worry that I'll give another moment's thought to it." She tilted her head and drawled, "I have been kissed before."

He didn't reply, didn't move. Only his eyes glittered in the moonlight as time stretched out and, growing increasingly edgy, she wondered whether he would ever take his leave or call her bluff and announce she might have been kissed, but never like *that*.

\* \* \*

Dear Reader,

Home is where the heart is. It's a great saying. One I believe in.

Unfortunately, sometimes choices aren't that simple.

Welcome back to Royal, home of the renowned Texas Cattleman's Club and a town set to erupt! In *Millionaire Playboy, Maverick Heiress,* the bid to claim the Club's presidency is heating up, gossip involving blue blood and babies is rife, and outsiders, like star-architect Daniel Warren, have been called in to shake up some stodgy foundations.

Daniel is happy to help his friend and presidential hopeful, Abigail Langley, develop a winning design for the new clubhouse…even if painful memories of growing up in the South has Daniel eager to jet back to New York as soon as business is done. He didn't bank on meeting Elizabeth Milton, a woman who holds his fascination as effortlessly as she combines a wardrobe of blue jeans and cowboy boots with furs and priceless jewels. A brief steamy affair seems inevitable. The subsequent choice between his heart and her home is far less cut and dried.

Hope you enjoy Daniel and Elizabeth's story!

With best wishes,

Robyn

ROBYN GRADY

# MILLIONAIRE PLAYBOY, MAVERICK HEIRESS

Special thanks and acknowledgment to Robyn Grady for her contribution to the Texas Cattleman's Club: The Showdown miniseries.

ISBN-13: 978-0-373-73127-5

MILLIONAIRE PLAYBOY, MAVERICK HEIRESS

Copyright © 2011 by Harlequin Books S.A.

This edition published by arrangement with Harlequin Books S.A.

For questions and comments about the quality of this book please contact us at Customer_eCare@Harlequin.ca.

www.Harlequin.com

**Printed in U.S.A.**

---

## *ROBYN GRADY*

was first published with Harlequin Books in 2007. Her books have since featured regularly on bestseller lists and at award ceremonies, including the National Readers' Choice Award, The Booksellers' Best Award, Cataromance Reviewers' Choice Award and Australia's prestigious Romantic Book of the Year Award.

Robyn lives on Queensland's beautiful Sunshine Coast with her real-life hero husband and three daughters. When she can be dragged away from tapping out her next story, Robyn visits the theater, the beach and the mall (a lot!). To keep fit she jogs (and shops) and dances with her youngest to Hannah Montana.

Robyn believes writing romance is the best job on the planet and she loves to hear from her readers. So drop by www.robyngrady.com and pass on your thoughts!

This story is dedicated to the talented authors
who also contributed to this series.

It's a *huge* honor. Thanks for having me along.

And to the series editor Charles Griemsman,
who is as fabulous as everyone says!

* * *

Don't miss a single book in this series!

**Texas Cattleman's Club: The Showdown**
*They are rich and powerful, hot and wild.*
*For these Texans, it's showdown time!*

# One

Just what was so funny?

Daniel Warren's focus dropped from the hot blonde sending over a half amused, half pitying look to the architectural model he and three of his design team were struggling to carry. Admittedly, the mock-up was large in more ways than one, but Texas was a big state. The new headquarters for the renowned Texas Cattleman's Club needed to make a big statement. Aesthetics like giant steer horns adorning a twenty-foot-high cowhide double entrance wasn't over the top.

Was it?

His second in charge, Rand Marks, spoke in his ear.

"Boss, this weighs a ton. Want to keep moving?"

From their expressions, the other assistants were also curious about the holdup. There wasn't one. Or shouldn't be.

Daniel was known in the business not only for talent but also decisiveness. He couldn't remember the last time he'd second-guessed himself. When he'd been invited to submit for this project, he'd put his fifteen odd years of successful industry know-how behind developing a design that would blow the committee members away—old-school as well as avant-garde. And yet now, that bombshell's one dubious look burned like a smoking brand in his mind.

Who was she anyway?

"I'm sorry to intrude, but you must be Abigail Langley's friend?"

At the sound of a sultry, Southern, very female voice, Daniel's heartbeat skipped and his attention shifted again. The blonde, and her ambivalent expression, now stood an arm's length away. Close up, she wasn't merely hot. Lord above, she was stunning. Wrapped up in a silver-fur jacket and jeans that hugged hips and thighs just right, she looked as if she'd just stepped off the Aspen slopes. Set in a fine oval face, large, well-lashed green eyes sparkled like a pair of priceless jewels. But her long bouncy mane struck him most. It was the kind of hair that made a man's fingertips itch to reach out and touch.

Setting his jaw, Daniel straightened his spine.

None of that altered the fact he was less than thrilled by her reaction to his work. He'd satisfied countless clients and had become filthy rich in the process. He didn't need to field subtle insults at the eleventh hour from "Miss Texas and Loving It" here.

Dragging his gaze from those plump kissable lips, Daniel cleared his throat and answered the lady's question.

"Yes. I'm Abigail Langley's friend—"

"Daniel Warren." She tasted his name as if she were enjoying a sip of sweet hot chocolate on a blustery winter's day. "You're the hotshot architect Abigail brought in all the way from New York City."

When the peak of one fair eyebrow arched, Daniel took a

moment. Was she goading or flirting? With these Southern belles, who could tell?

"Don't know about hotshot, but I'm well-known in the industry," he confirmed as her weight shifted from one denim-clad leg to the other and she hitched her Birkin higher on one shoulder. "You know Abigail, too?"

"Everyone in these parts knows Abby. Her husband, God rest his soul, was the great-great-great-grandson of Tex Langley, the founder of this establishment." When she leaned a conspiratorial inch closer, he caught the scent of her perfume—delicate with undertones of dangerous. "My money's on Abigail to win the upcoming election. She'd make a fine club president—" those lush lips pursed "—no matter what that stick-in-the-mud Brad Price has to say on the matter."

A suit in his forties sauntered up. He spared Daniel a cursory glance before addressing the lady with a lazy Texan drawl.

"My dear, we're expected inside."

"I was introducing myself to a visitor to Royal," she said, indicating Daniel with a nod and interested smile.

"Boss?"

Daniel's attention slid back. Damn, he'd forgotten the boys.

"If you're going to be a while," Rand said, "mind if the rest of us take this inside? Don't know about you but my arms are ready to snap."

Daniel slipped his arms from beneath the model's base as the other three continued on up the path to the headquarters' front doors.

Daniel wiped his palms down his trousers then offered his hand. "Daniel Warren."

"Elizabeth Milton." Her hand was small and warm but her grip defied the term *weaker sex*. "And this is Chadwick Tremain."

Her escort offered a curt nod and, without accepting Daniel's extended hand, wound his arm through Elizabeth Milton's.

"Mr. Warren," he muttered in acknowledgment. Then to Elizabeth, "Our table's waiting."

She glanced over her shoulder as his team disappeared through the headquarters' opened doors. Then, looking back at her companion, she angled her head, sending that blond waterfall cascading like a sheet of silk over one shoulder. "Y'all go on ahead, Chad. I'll catch up."

The man's salt-and-pepper eyebrows knitted. "I told Michaels we'd be—"

"Chad." She unwound her arm from his. "I'll meet you inside."

Daniel thought he heard the older man growl before he straightened the Windsor knot at his throat and sauntered away.

Daniel grunted. "Your boyfriend doesn't like me much."

"Boyfriend?" Those emeralds sparkled as she laughed. "Chad's my financial advisor. He keeps an eye out for me."

"You need looking after?"

A faint line creased between her eyebrows. "I suppose that's a matter of opinion," she said, before placing one cowboy boot in front of the other and heading at a leisurely pace up the path. "You sound like a Yankee, Mr. Warren." She grinned at his custom-made black wool overcoat. "You dress like one, too. But I detect a hint of South Carolina in your accent."

While Daniel's throat swelled, he maintained his unaffected air. It had been years since his move. His escape. Few picked up on the remnants of a drawl anymore.

"These days, home's a long way from Charleston," he offered.

"You don't miss the—"

"No," he cut in with a quick smile. "I don't."

New York was just far enough away from the South and its memories. The only reason he was down this far was business, and as soon as that was concluded he'd roll his sleeves back down and red-eye it home to the life he'd built and loved.

"I hope you plan on seeing a little of our state while you're here," she went on as they strolled side by side.

"Famous for the Alamo, ten-gallon hats and, uh, long-horns."

Her lips twitched at his leading look and inflection on his last word. "Oh, your design's not entirely bad."

He wanted to ask her what, in her opinion, would make a good design. Which was crazy. Firstly, he was the guy with the credentials and, secondly, he didn't need to complicate his limited time here by musing over someone who was, perhaps, ten years his junior and whose loyalty no doubt lay in her daddy's oil fields and memories of the wild, Wild West.

Definitely not his scene.

Entering the club's foyer, which was all dark wood and old-world smells and charm, he stopped to bid his little-known companion goodbye. But Elizabeth Milton's attention had drifted elsewhere, to a sign hung over the entrance door.

"Abigail would've told you about this?" she asked.

He examined the iron-studded plaque and read the words burned into the wood. "Leadership, Justice and Peace."

"The Texas Cattleman's creed," she explained reverently. "The words are strong enough without the legend that brought them together." Her gaze caught his, so wide and innocent that something in his chest swelled to twice its size then fisted tight. "You ought to get Abigail to tell you the story. It might give you something to work with."

Daniel's jaw shifted. He could take that comment as a slight. And yet every cell in his body urged him to put pride aside and listen up. If there was an anecdote behind the plaque that might help with his design, who better to relay it than someone who could combine those boots, which were only missing their spurs, with a ten-thousand-dollar coat and somehow make it work.

Only now Elizabeth Milton's attention, as she wound out of her fur, had veered toward the dining room. Mr. Tremain, and the lasso he liked looped around his client's waist, was waiting.

"Perhaps I'll see you around," Daniel said.

Her beautiful smile was wry. "I'm around most of the time."

When she tipped her head, preparing to leave, that something lurking in Daniel's chest looped and tugged all the tighter. In another time and place, he'd have asked if she'd care to join him for a drink. Instead, he merely returned the smile when she said, "Good luck, Mr. Warren. Hope you enjoy your time in Royal."

He watched those sinful jeans sashay away beneath a dark timber lintel. That woman might be Texan to her core, but she sure as heck didn't walk like she spent most of her time on a horse. In fact, she moved with the finesse of a runway model, with the fluid grace of a cat.

A smile hooked one corner of his mouth.

Yeah. Elizabeth Milton sure was something.

A heartbeat before she disappeared around that corner, he said to hell with it and called out, "Miss Milton!"

Shimmering blond arced out as she spun around and stepped back into his direct line of sight. Winding out of his own coat, he stepped forward.

"I wondered if you can recommend a good place to eat. Aside from here, I mean."

Those gorgeous green eyes flashed. "I could recommend several, Mr. Warren."

"In that case, would you consider joining me for dinner? I'd be interested to hear that story."

Her teeth worried her lower lip as one hand went behind and, he imagined, slid into a back jeans pocket.

"On one condition," she announced.

"That we don't discuss building plans?"

She laughed, a melodic sound that soaked into his pores and eased his smile wider. "To the contrary. I'd very much like to discuss possibilities for your design."

"Then we simply need the venue."

"Twenty miles down the main road on your left at, let's say, seven?"

"The name of the establishment?"

"Milton Ranch."

He did a double take. "You're inviting me to dinner at your house?"

"Trust me, Mr. Warren." She pivoted around and, hand still cupped low in that pocket, spoke over her shoulder as she moved off. "I believe you'll find the experience most rewarding."

As Elizabeth entered the Cattleman's Club dining room, a few people nearest the entrance glanced up from their meals or pre-luncheon drinks. She'd grown up knowing a great many of these folk, and anyone whose eye caught hers offered a warm smile.

At one time she'd rebelled against the idea of spending the majority of her time in Royal. Now, that seemed so long ago. In reality it had been only four years since her parents' deaths and her own life had taken a sharp turn. But, frankly, she was grateful for the legal roadblocks her mother and father had erected to help steer her against a course she would likely have taken—a course that would have led her away from her roots.

If she breached the terms of their will by spending more than two months away from home during any twelve-month period, she would forfeit the majority of her inheritance, not merely the ranch but also, she'd come to realize, a good portion of her identity—who she was and continued wanting to be.

Still she couldn't deny that meeting Daniel Warren just now had more than rekindled her interest in places beyond these borders. Daniel was different, Elizabeth decided as she handed her coat to the maître d'. Amusing. Dark and polished and New York cool. Abigail had said her visiting architect was extremely successful. He'd have traveled widely and often. A man of the world.

Not that she opposed good Texan stock, Elizabeth noted, heading for her usual table in a far corner by a row of windows. In fact, when the time came to start a family, her partner would more likely than not hail from these parts. At the very least he'd appreciate her situation and stand one hundred percent behind her commitment to keep the Milton Ranch. Which ruled out hotshot architects from up North.

Although, God knows, that boy was cute.

Chad pushed to his feet as she skirted around the remaining tables.

"I was about to see what was keeping you," he said, retracting her chair.

"I'm not going anywhere," she replied in a sweet but pointed tone.

"I was only—"

"I know you were *only.*"

She swallowed that spike of irritation and calmly collected the menu. But Chad wasn't prepared to let it go.

"Elizabeth, it's my duty to watch out for you."

"I'm not a child," she reminded him. She'd been twenty-one when he'd been handed, via the will, the role of her financial advisor. But she was older now, wiser and far more responsible.

"Your parents only had your best interests at heart when they included that caveat and put me in charge."

He leaned closer, about to say more, when the waiter arrived and took their orders—steak for him, pecan and avocado salad for her. Chad was looking thoughtful, pouring iced tea, when he spoke next.

"That man—Mr. Warren…"

"Abigail Langley's architect." Relishing a grin, Elizabeth reached for her glass. "I can't wait to see the results of that election come December."

Chad scoffed. "If Abigail expects votes to swing her way because of an eyesore of a design like that, she's dreaming more than I'd thought."

Elizabeth wouldn't touch his comment about the design. "I'm sure the majority commend the committee for awarding Abigail full membership privileges after her husband passed away. She has as much right as any member to stand for president. If it weren't for her late husband's ancestors, there wouldn't be a Texas Cattleman's Club," she said.

"At the risk of sounding sexist, it's not the Cattleperson's Club."

"Perhaps it ought to be."

"Change isn't always good, Elizabeth. Sometimes it can lead to discord. To ruin."

And sometimes it was necessary. Even exciting. But she wouldn't waste her breath. Instead, her cheeks warm from building annoyance, she took a long sip of cool tea.

"Have you and Mr. Warren met before?"

"No." She set her glass on the table.

"He seems a smooth sort."

She grinned again. "Yes, he does."

"I don't trust him."

Enough. She met Chad Tremain's gaze square on.

"You were a dear friend of my parents, I count you as a friend of mine, but drop it." She forced a short laugh to temper her tone. "Okay?"

"It's just… Elizabeth, you know that I care."

His fingers edged over the table. Her stomach knotting, Elizabeth slid her hand away and locked both sets of fingers in her lap. Yes, she knew Chad cared, far more than she would have liked. He was too serious and staid and not her type at all. Couldn't he see she wasn't interested?

In fact, despite her parents' wishes, if there were any way to dismiss him as her financial advisor she'd do it. However, for now at least, she was hog-tied. The terms of the will were set until her thirtieth birthday. Sitting here now and feeling inordinately constrained, it might as well be her sixtieth.

Needing to change the subject, she cast a glance around the buzzing room. "Where's Mr. Michaels?" Her bank manager.

Sitting back, Chad nodded at his cell phone, placed on the other side of his cutlery.

"Detained. I thought we could review the figures of those larger annuities while we wait."

Elizabeth sipped tea and listened as Chad spouted off strings of figures, but after a few minutes, his voice seemed to blend with other sounds—glasses pinging, cutlery clicking, people chatting, laughing. And suddenly, through the condensation of the pitcher that sat at the center of their table, a face swam up.

Glossy dark hair. A hint of Latin heritage, perhaps. Sea-green eyes full of questions and possibilities. Then there was the confident air that exuded strength but also cloaked a more vulnerable side, if she weren't mistaken. She barely knew Daniel Warren and yet something very real about him made her heart beat faster than a piston hammering at full throttle.

What would Chad say if he knew she'd gone and asked him to dinner?

"Elizabeth?"

Starting, she snapped her attention back to her luncheon companion.

"I'm sorry, Chad. What was that?"

"I thought I'd mention that we received another offer to buy the ranch. Developers, of course. I took it upon myself to tell the gentleman the property was not for sale."

She contained a sigh. "Thank you, but I can deal with those inquiries myself. Even if I were in a position to sell, I know where my heart lies."

At least, now she did.

The words were barely out when movement beyond the nearby window caught her eye. Daniel Warren was strolling the manicured grounds with a concerned-looking Abigail. When he turned toward the window and Elizabeth imagined he'd noticed her looking through the pane, her stomach jumped and flipped over. Holding her breath, she lowered her head even as a runaway smile stole across her face.

She was looking forward to tonight like she hadn't looked forward to anything in a long time.

"My dear? Are you all right?"

Crunching her napkin, Elizabeth focused on the older man's face, which was lined with curiosity. Or was that suspicion?

"I was saying that I know where my heart lies." She pushed thoughts of Daniel Warren aside, replaced them with an image of the Milton Ranch and affirmed, "And that's right here in Royal."

# Two

That evening, as Daniel swerved his rental SUV around the top of the Milton Ranch graveled driveway, his breath caught in his throat at the same time his mouth dropped open.

Usually in this kind of situation, before anything else, professional instinct demanded an immediate once-over of the house—its position, angles, any interesting textures and touches. Tonight, however, the sprawling homestead, set on too many acres of prime land to imagine, didn't come close to drawing his attention. Instead, his focus was riveted on the scene illuminated by recently triggered lawn lights. Easing out of the vehicle, he rubbed his eyes and looked harder.

Flamingos?

The pink-and-white imitation birds were strategically positioned beneath the benevolent arms of a glorious magnolia. Daniel scrubbed the back of his neck. Hell, maybe Elizabeth Milton's success with that eclectic ensemble today was a fluke, after all.

"You're on time."

Daniel swung around to see Elizabeth standing, a shoulder propped against the jamb of the massive doorway of her home. The cowboy boots she'd worn earlier had been replaced by elegant black heels, which matched an equally elegant little black dress. The blond mane was swept up in an effortless, chic style. Her arms were wrapped around her waist and a mock curious smile shone from her face. Beneath the porch lights, her every inch glowed. The only anomaly was the double foxtail belt loosely slung around her hips.

Daniel looked at it sideways but, after those pink birds, he couldn't decide. Was the belt high or hillbilly fashion?

"Are you going to stand there all night, Mr. Warren? It might be October but it's chilly out."

"I was admiring your, uh, landscaping."

"The flamingos? Attractive, aren't they?" When he found himself tongue-tied, she straightened to her full petite height and laughed. "They're only on loan, silly. A gimmick to raise money for a very good cause. They show up one morning and you get to mind them until you make a donation, at which time they magically disappear and take up residence with a new and unsuspecting victim."

Closing the vehicle's door, he blew out a sigh of relief. "Making that donation must be at the top of your to-do list."

As he joined her, his senses responded to that same sweet scent he'd enjoyed earlier today. His every extremity warmed, urging him to lean closer to her pulse points and inhale. But almost as captivating was another kind of smell, one that sent his taste buds tripping. Man, he hadn't realized he was that hungry.

"You've been busy in the kitchen?"

She stepped aside and ushered him into a vestibule that was decorated with oak and a striking stacked-slate feature wall.

"I'm under direct orders to leave all the cooking to the

expert in this house," she said, accepting his coat and slipping it into a hall closet. "Nita's been a member of the staff, a member of the family, since before I was in pigtails. I couldn't do without her."

She led him into a reception room, furnished with evergreen and crimson window dressings and impressive Jacobean furniture. But his interest soon slid back to the way his hostess filled out that dress. Frankly, the sight of her legs in sheer black stockings made his head swim a little, foxtails or not.

"Can I interest you in a predinner drink?" she asked, leaving him to cross to a mile-long timber bar. Beneath the lights, tiny diamantés sparkled in her hair. With a teasing grin, she held up a bottle of whiskey and suggested, "A Manhattan, perhaps?"

Grinning, he sauntered over. "Thanks, but I wouldn't say no to a beer."

When in Rome... Didn't all Texans love their ale?

"In that case—" she pulled a frosty beer from under the counter "—a local coming up."

"Will you join me?"

"I'm more a bubbles gal." When she lifted an opened bottle, nesting in a nearby silver ice bucket, he studied and openly approved the label.

"A very fine vintage."

"You know wines." It was more a statement than a question.

"I know what's good." Clearly so did she.

"Two glasses then?"

"I'll pour."

She found a pair of cut-crystal flutes. He filled one, handed hers over then filled his own. When she tilted her head and raised her glass, diamonds seemed to sparkle in her eyes as well as her hair.

"A toast," she said. "To your design helping Abby bag the election."

His chest tightened and the glass stopped halfway to his mouth. "Only if I put it through a massive overhaul."

Understanding shone in her eyes. "Abigail didn't like it?"

"She was too polite to say but I'm sure she hated it. Turns out I took a bit of a bum steer regarding the theme, courtesy of a plant from her opponent's camp."

"Brad Price doesn't mind playing dirty."

Her growl sounded more like a kitten than a bear, although he didn't doubt that beneath all that feminine grace lay the heart of a tiger.

"What did Abby say?"

He wouldn't go into details. "Suffice to say her expression was enough."

Images of his design rolled through his head, his thoughts working through the exterior structure then the overly rustic properties of each room. He could see where he'd gone wrong now.

"Too many textures and dimensions harking back to the good ol' days," he admitted. "Too stereotypical."

Damn it, too cheesy. His fingertip began to draw geometrical shapes over the counter. Helped him to think.

"I get that the committee wants to retain the club's original flavor," he went on, "while positioning it firmly in the twenty-first century. I need to find that balance."

Elizabeth rounded the timber counter and didn't stop until her heavenly scent had claimed his personal space and was hijacking his bloodstream. The impulse to edge closer and breathe a little deeper was something he had to work at to contain.

An eyebrow arched, she rested her crystal flute on her chin while those dazzling smoky-shadowed eyes searched his. "You sound as if you might have a few ideas."

"Earlier today, so did you."

"I confess, I do possess a fascination for design."

"You studied it?"

"Not officially."

She rotated to lean back against the counter. With her weight preferring one shapely leg, elbows propped up on the counter on either side, she looked so sultry, so classic... Hell, if he'd been an artist, he'd have begged for an easel and brush.

"I have majors in psychology and literature," she told him.

"I'd have guessed a business degree would've been the logical choice, given one day you'd be running all this."

Besides other things, when he'd inquired, Abigail had told him Elizabeth was an only child.

Some of the light in her eyes waned at the same time her gaze dropped to the original polished timber at her feet. "I wasn't that interested in the ranch back then. When my folks passed away, I began to see things differently. There's always time for more study."

He set his glass carefully down. "Abigail mentioned about your parents." A tragic automobile accident. "I'm sorry."

She nodded then shucked back her slender shoulders. "How about you, Mr. Warren? Do you have family?"

Daniel's insides knotted. Given the thread of their conversation, it was an obvious question. Now he would avoid giving a straight answer, because he didn't discuss that facet of his life. His past. Not with anyone.

Before he could maneuver the conversation in another direction, they were interrupted.

"Sorry to barge in, folks."

Daniel rotated toward the accented female voice. A woman, late sixties in a printed apron and matching slippers, was taking her time crossing the room.

"Just wanta say," the woman said, peering at Daniel

through lenses that covered a good deal of her face, "dinner's on the table."

Elizabeth moved to join her. "Nita Ramirez, this is Mr. Warren. The architect from New York City I told you about."

"Please, Elizabeth, Nita, the name's Daniel." Making his way over, he extended a hand, which Nita Ramirez readily shook—and for quite a time. "I hear you're a fabulous talent in the kitchen," Daniel added.

Nita patted her jet-black shoulder-length hair. "That compliment'll earn you a second helping of my specialty dessert, Daniel. How does caramel apple cheesecake sound?"

He almost licked his lips. "My sweet tooth and I can hardly wait."

Pleased, Nita sent over a hearty wink then spoke to Elizabeth. "Dining room's all set, Beth. I set a match to the fire, too."

As Nita strolled off, Elizabeth offered her arm to her guest. "I sure hope you're hungry."

At the end of the meal, Elizabeth dabbed the corners of her mouth with her napkin, to hide her grin more than anything. A man of Daniel's means would dine at the best restaurants around the world, and while guests regularly swooned over Nita's culinary triumphs, her current guest's reaction to rib eye roast and baked potato salad was priceless. No question. Daniel Warren appreciated good home cooking.

"I'm sure there's more," Elizabeth offered, "if you can fit it in."

He set his knife and fork down on the gravy-smeared plate. "I'm tempted. But I need room for that dessert."

"Be warned. Caramel apple cheesecake is addictive."

"I'm an advocate of the saying, you can never have too much of a good thing."

When his gaze held hers a moment longer than was

necessary, heat climbed up Elizabeth's neck and she had to drop her gaze, catch her breath. She wasn't one to titter. She didn't normally blush like a schoolgirl when a man flirted. But, sitting here with Daniel, she felt something new, unexpected and highly pleasurable playing tag with her senses.

As they'd talked through dinner—about music, politics, how cool the weather was for this time of year—her awareness of every facet of his presence had grown until the buzz she'd felt from the moment they'd met had cranked up to high. Whenever he looked at her the way he had just now, all over her skin, through her blood, she tingled. Frankly, she wanted to surrender to a long sigh and fan herself.

With Daniel Warren she felt as much like a teenage girl as a woman.

When the tips of her breasts began to harden and heat, clearing her thoughts, Elizabeth set down her napkin and inhaled a leveling breath. Get back on track. He was looking forward to dessert.

"I'm guessing you don't cook," she said, fighting the urge to cross her arms, contain that heat.

"Not much." Sheepish, he tugged his ear. "Not at all."

"And there I was, imagining you sweating over a gas cooker, tossing the escargot."

His mouth turned down. "You like snails?"

"I've indulged, but only when I visit a particular café on the Rue de la Villette." As his eyebrows knitted and he gave a curious grin, she cocked her head. "You've been to Paris?"

"Me? Sure. Beautiful city. Although it's always good to get back home."

"To the States?"

"To New York."

Elizabeth almost forgot herself and frowned. Nothing wrong with being precise. Still, if she hadn't known better, she might think that reply was pointed. That perhaps Abigail had clued him up on more than her parents' misfortune. That she might have confided in her situation with regard to that condition of their will.

Which was crazy. Abigail wouldn't break that kind of confidence, and he couldn't have found out anywhere else— Chad Tremain, for example. Obviously her thoughts—those sensations he stirred—were running away on her, filling her head with fancies.

Elizabeth set her mind back on the conversation.

"New York has some incredible restaurants."

He ran an appreciative eye over his plate. "None that serve food like that."

"Is your mother a good cook?"

His smile froze for a heartbeat before he reached for his wine. "Mom could cook."

"Do your parents still live in Carolina?"

"No." He pushed back his chair and glanced around as he took a mouthful of red and swallowed. "The decor in here is interesting."

"Early American," she replied, thinking not of furniture but the fact he'd avoided talking about his family. Before dinner he'd hesitated when she'd inquired. Although she and her parents had been close, estrangement between generations wasn't uncommon. But she wouldn't push. Private was private. Even if she was more than curious.

They were talking about decor.

"My mother redecorated parts of this house, but not this room. She liked it homey. The dinner table is where the family comes together, she used to say. Not only to eat, but to talk and listen and plan."

Daniel's smile held. "A wonderful, traditional concept." His attention wandered to the far wall. "Those dark wood panels are almost identical to the club's."

"Might've been cut from the same tree. Heck, the ranch and the club have both been around since Buffalo Bill was a boy."

He pretended to pull his head in. "Do I detect a hint of impatience?"

Amused, she blinked twice. "Why on earth would you say that?"

"That resigned note in your voice."

"That wasn't a resigned note."

"Sounded pretty clear to me—"

"You were mistaken." She lifted her chin. "What you heard was respect."

"So you don't harbor any secret plans to turn the ranch into a casino or suburban lots like some others down this way?"

She coughed out a laugh even as heat crept up her neck again, this time for a different reason. Was he serious?

"What a curious thing to say. Of course not."

"But you would like some change," he went on. "Am I right?"

With a practiced smile, she set her elbow on the chair's arm and fiddled with her diamond drop earring. "Is your sideline mind reading, Mr. Warren?"

"It's Daniel, remember?"

Knowing an edge had crept into her voice, Elizabeth played up her smile. She didn't like his line of thought. His questions. Her ideas on tradition—when, where and how to tweak— were her business, just as whatever prickled Daniel about his family's past was his.

But she'd answer his question—in her own way.

"While it's time the Cattleman's Club challenged some of its older trappings, I can't see Milton Ranch changing. My parents wanted tradition to live on here." She reached for her glass. "So do I."

Regardless of the will, she would never sell, especially to developers.

Still, truth was, she wished she had some middle-of-the-road option. Just a little more freedom...

"Who's up for dessert?"

Elizabeth snapped back from her thoughts. Nita had entered the room, ready to clear the plates. Daniel held his stomach, which Elizabeth wouldn't mind betting was a six-pack.

"I might let that delicious roast settle first," he said, handing over his plate. "That was a big helping."

"A man deserves to be satisfied at the end of the day."

At the housekeeper's last comment, Elizabeth shot her a glare. Nita only returned an innocent grin. The Milton Ranch housekeeper was a well-known matchmaker, but if she was hoping to set up the toll of wedding bells tonight, Nita could put her scheming mind to rest. As far as sexual attraction was concerned, Daniel Warren was a big fat ten, but he was passing through. He might even have a girl back home in New York. Maybe two. And while marriage was a definite in her future, Elizabeth wasn't after long-term just now. Hell, she was only twenty-five.

Plates in hand, almost at the doorway, Nita suggested, "You ought to go for a walk. Help work off that meal."

Elizabeth pushed to her feet. "I'm sure Daniel would prefer to take in more of the house." See if anything inspired ideas for his project.

But as her guest unfolded to his full height, he gifted her with a deliciously sinful smile. "I like Nita's idea." He offered his arm. "Let's go work it off."

Ten minutes later, as he and Elizabeth made their way down a graveled path that led to the Milton Ranch stables, Daniel stole a glance at his companion's dusty yard boots—

the Jimmy Choos had been deemed unsuitable—and the bulky work coat thrown over her stunning black evening dress. Then he studied her perfect profile, highlighted by the rising moon's silver beams, and decided Elizabeth Milton would exude panache wearing a brown paper bag. "Eclectic" suited her, like he couldn't imagine it suiting any other. She achieved real style effortlessly when, in his experience, females often tried too hard to look their best, be the best. That last wasn't a gender-specific phenomenon, particularly amidst the never-ending bustle and hustle of New York.

Daniel's focus lifted to the sky.

But Milton Ranch was a long way from those city lights. Damn, he'd never seen so many stars.

"How much land have you got here?" he asked.

"Three thousand acres," Elizabeth replied, pride evident in her voice as she dug her hands into her coat pockets.

"Must be a challenge."

"One I'm prepared to face. Although rising costs and lack of trained hands make it difficult," she admitted.

"But you're in for the long haul."

"My parents left money enough to keep the tradition going. Ranching is in my blood."

A vision of Elizabeth at five years of age wearing an Annie Oakley costume, charging off toward an endless horizon on her very own pony, made him smile.

"So you grew up learning how to rope a steer?" he asked as they crunched farther down the shadowed path.

"I was a cowgirl but only in between attending boarding school."

"A school close to home?"

"Initially in Houston. In my teens, overseas. Switzerland, France."

"Where you dined on sautéed mollusks." *Snails.*

"Helix pomatia, to be precise," she said with mock authority.

He lifted an eyebrow. "My, sounds like those boarding schools didn't waste your parents' money."

"I received a great education. Had some wonderful experiences. Made some lifelong friends." And in her faraway expression he could see she wouldn't say no to a sojourn to Europe right this minute. He could well imagine her expertly skiing Alpine slopes, wandering around the history and culture of the Louvre.

"Bet you're on and off jets, visiting all the time."

Before the moon disappeared behind a cloud, he saw her smile waver but, a moment later, her shoulders in that big coat rolled back.

"There's a lot to keep me busy here."

Daniel's step faltered. Here was a beautiful, obviously intelligent woman with mega funds at her disposal. She'd beamed speaking about that Parisian café, about her experiences overseas and the friends she'd made there. She was young, which translated into plenty of energy and enthusiasm, the kind she showed for this ranch. Had he misinterpreted or had she as good as confessed she didn't get out much?

Just how much of her time did this ranch take up?

"I guess the responsibility of three thousand acres is a lot," he prodded as the silhouette of the stables loomed before them.

"I have people to manage matters, although more and more I'd rather handle things myself."

He shot over a glance. "Really?"

A strand of blond escaped its upsweep and danced in the breeze as she frowned. "Why so surprised?"

"To be honest—" he shrugged "—practically everything about you surprises me."

She sent him a saucy grin. "Good."

A moment later, a whinny sounded as they approached the stable's single side door.

"This building replaced the original stable a decade ago," she said, shifting the catch. "We had a fire. No horses lost, thank heaven. When Dad upgraded, he made sure it was with the best materials and safety features."

Stepping inside, she flicked a light switch then pointed out a framed photograph, hanging on the wall, of a grand turn-of-the-previous-century red timber barn.

"This one doesn't smell the same," she said, "doesn't have the same feel, but it's easier to keep clean and has loads more space."

As the smell of fresh hay and horse filled his lungs, Daniel concurred. This was a clean wide structure, with two-dozen individual stalls, as well as windows and a skylight that would allow in an ideal amount of natural light during the day. Not the personality of the old post-and-beam barn with its massive hayloft, but far more practical.

Times change.

Elizabeth crossed to the first stall on the left. Hooves pawed at a straw floor, then came a welcoming snort, a sound that made Daniel smile and wish his father had listened to him for once and let him learn how to ride. Hunting was Judge Buck Warren's passion. Daniel still hadn't forgiven his father for that.

Elizabeth arrived at the stall gate. A regal-looking horse, with a glossy black coat and mane, greeted her by nudging its muzzle against her shoulder. Elizabeth, so small against this other's height and might, seemed to come alive as she scrubbed her palm over its cheek and murmured words that had Daniel longing to be on the receiving end.

Her face filled with adoration, she looked over. "This is Ame Sœur."

"Kindred Spirit."

For the first time he noticed a delicate dimple either side of her smile. "I'll have you eating escargot yet."

He pretended to shudder. "You two seem good friends."

"The best," she said, and the horse blew through his lips as if to agree. "We try to saddle up every day."

"Unless you're away."

The motion of her hand stroking his muzzle stopped while she fished into her coat pocket and extracted a huge red apple. Her horse's head reared back as his lips wobbled, searching out the treat. He was crunching into the fruit when she replied in a somber tone.

"Daniel, did Abby say something to you?"

"Say something? About what?"

Searching his eyes, she seemed to consider his response before she dropped her gaze then refocused on the horse, which was chomping and nudging for more. "Nothing. It's nothing."

When he moved closer, she pulled another apple from her pocket. "Want to feed him?"

"Maybe later."

"We mostly use trucks and bikes these days." The horse bit into the second apple. "But if I check the stock and fences, I like to do it with Ame."

"Right now I'm interested in what you think Abigail might have told me."

He couldn't believe it was anything sinister. So what was it that had this normally poised woman looking suddenly flustered?

Still, whatever it was didn't concern him…unless she wanted it to.

He tilted his head. "And if you want me to back off, say the word."

With those diamond drops sparkling beneath the fluorescents, she looked him square on for a deliberative moment then finally blew out a breath.

"My parents included a caveat in their will," she said. "I'm obliged to stay here, in Royal, a good deal of any given year."

He frowned. "What do you mean—a good deal?"

"I get two months to travel outside of Royal."

He took a moment to digest the ramifications. "And if you're gone for, say, two months and one day?"

"I forfeit my inheritance."

He wanted to laugh. "You're kidding, right? You lose the ranch?"

"There are reasons—"

"The reason is called blackmail."

Disgust flooded her face. "My parents didn't blackmail me."

"What do you call it when someone threatens to take away what you care about if you don't do exactly what they want?"

Hell, he was an expert on the subject. How many times growing up had he heard one or the other of his divorced parents say, "Daniel, you won't see your mother/father again if you don't…" Fill in the blank. By the end of it, he didn't care if he ever saw either one of them again.

Her fists plowed into those coat pockets at the same time her chin kicked up. "It's not blackmail. It's called handing down responsibility."

Poor, misguided Miss Milton, Daniel thought, and slowly shook his head.

"You are young, aren't you."

Her eyes flashed. "I'm as much an adult, and in charge of my life, as you are."

"That's why you're still doing what your parents tell you."

She studied him with eyes that burned.

"Do you come from this kind of background?"

His shoulders went back. "I refused to have anything to

do with my parents' money." Their bribes. He was a self-made man.

"You shunned your parents?" Her tone was pitying. "No. Of course you wouldn't understand."

"I understand you're kidding yourself if you think you're in charge of your life," he said. "Way I see it, you're walking around in chains most of the time." To a homebody, the caveat might not seem like a hardship. But Elizabeth made no secret of the fact she loved to travel. Explore new lands. Meet new people. She was energetic and, God knew, she had the means. But what good was money if she was forbidden from using it the way she'd most like? Elizabeth hadn't been given a choice, like he hadn't been given a choice when he was growing up. Being helpless—voiceless—had to be the worst feeling in the world.

"Is that why you don't see your parents, Daniel?" she asked calmly. "Because you don't like chains? Don't like ties? Because you wanted to be in charge?"

He gave a jaded smile as emotion filled his chest. Elizabeth Milton knew nothing about him. He was wrong to have pushed. Wrong to have wanted to get involved.

"It's been a great evening," he told her in a level no-hard-feelings tone. "It's time I got back."

Her mouth uncharacteristically tight, she nodded. "I'm sure you need to rise early, as do I."

"Thank Nita for the meal."

"Good luck with your future endeavors."

"I'll walk you back to the house."

"No need. I've walked that path so often, I'd know it in a tornado."

She was welcome to it.

He moved out of the stables, heard her close the door. Head down, he'd taken a half-dozen steps when she called out.

"Daniel. I want you to know, I'm happy staying here,"

she told him as he turned around. "Sometimes it's a little… inconvenient. But I've come to see this ranch is my future."

"That's fine." Totally her business. He tipped his head. "Good night."

He'd begun to turn away when she interrupted again.

"You don't believe me."

"It shouldn't matter what I believe."

"It's only until I turn thirty."

By thirty he'd been well on his way to being successful, and happy, in his own right. But, again, not his concern.

"You don't have to convince me."

"I don't want you to leave feeling sorry for me," she pointed out. "I have everything any person could want or need."

"Just make sure you don't include freedom on that list."

She growled, "It's not a restriction."

"No?"

"No."

As she stood before him, defiant in the moonlight, his skin heated, muscles clenched, and as his gaze held hers, a dark, deep urge overwhelmed him, a primitive impulse that set his heart pumping all the more. She didn't want his pity and, God save him, he didn't want to show her any. But she wanted him to believe she wasn't interested in too much beyond this parcel of land?

Miss Milton was a liar.

Prepared to tell her just that, he moved forward. He stopped an arm's length away, searched her questioning eyes but then, rather than speak, he acted, circling her waist and bringing her mercilessly close. At the same time he pressed her in and her mouth opened to protest, his head came down, lowering, determined, over hers.

While her hands bunched and pushed against his chest, he held her. When muffled, incensed noises vibrated from her throat, he didn't relent. Damn it, if he was going, he wanted to leave them both with at least a taste of what he'd felt bubbling and fermenting between them. He needed to show this woman what she already knew.

There was more to life than two months a year.

And gradually, as he'd known she would, Elizabeth came around to his way of thinking. Her fists loosened against his shirt until her fingertips were clinging rather than pushing him away. Her body, instead of objecting, relaxed and, bit by bit, dissolved. Best of all, her lips grew supple and parted, no longer refusing but inviting him in. Daniel smiled to himself.

Damn, it was good to be right.

But at the same moment his palms sculpted over and winged her shoulders in, Daniel also recognized a sliver of concern.

He couldn't get involved like this with Elizabeth Milton, particularly now.

What the hell had he begun?

# Three

As Elizabeth melted against that amazing wall of heat, she couldn't hold on to a thought, other than to know that this caress went above and beyond any she'd ever experienced, in real life or in dreams.

As Daniel's strong arms urged her closer and her palms filed up beneath his coat and over the solid scope of his chest, she absorbed every ounce of the magic. Her heart beat so fast she feared it would burst any moment. He'd unleashed such a torrent of emotion from so deep inside she could barely get enough air.

Elizabeth sighed in her throat.

Daniel Warren kissed like a god.

As hot fingertips massaged her nape, with a teasing lack of speed, his mouth gradually left hers. Now was the time she should open her eyes, demand to know what the hell he thought he was doing, pouncing on her like that, forcing her to succumb. But that delicious syrupy feeling humming through veins was just so fine. She felt as if she were floating two feet off the ground. As if her blood were singing. That Daniel Warren was practically a stranger, as well as someone who could never empathize with her situation, didn't quite register through the haze.

She only wanted him to kiss her again.

"Elizabeth?"

His voice was a husky whisper at her ear. The slide of his palm around her cheek left her trembling and leaning more into his touch. She felt the warmth of his breath on her forehead, on her temple. On reflex, her lips parted again and her face tipped toward his.

"Elizabeth, I can't say I didn't want to do that," he murmured in a drugging, deep voice. "Doesn't mean I should have."

His words swirled around through her mind until, little by little, their meaning took hold. Then, all at once, her chest squeezed and eyes snapped open. He was looking at her, gaze dark with regret. In that moment, the reality of what he'd done, what she'd let him do, flooded Elizabeth's senses until she prayed for the ground to open up and swallow her whole.

Good Lord, what must he think of her? One minute they were enmeshed in a heated discussion, the next she was twining herself around him like a clingy summer vine. Like a teenager her first time out necking. Elizabeth Milton was known not only for her spirit but also her decorum, and yet this man ignited fires within her that had reduced her to little more than a puddle. She'd never felt more vulnerable.

More alive.

Sucking in a breath, she dropped her arms, which had remained around his neck, and took an awkward step back. As his heat receded, the cool of the shadowed night enveloped her. Trembling, she drew her coat close.

"No need to apologize," she said in a thick voice. Avoiding his gaze, she shrugged. "Sometimes, when emotions run high, things happen."

"I want you to know, I don't make a habit of dragging women into my arms like that." He ran a hand through his hair, looked around. Out the corner of her eye, she saw him crack a lame smile. "Must be something in the air."

She closed her eyes and withered. If she could turn back time and wipe out these past few moments, she'd do it in a blink. That she'd surrendered so completely was bad enough. Did he need to rub in the fact that he regretted it, too?

"Daniel, please don't worry that I'll give another moment's thought to it." She tilted her head and drawled, "I have been kissed before."

He didn't reply, didn't move. Only his eyes glittered in the moonlight as time stretched out and, growing increasingly edgy, she wondered whether he would ever leave or call her bluff and announce she might have been kissed, but never like that.

But then he exhaled, took a look back over his shoulder toward the house and nodded once before he walked away. "Take care."

Her pulse beating in her ears, Elizabeth watched Daniel walk away down the path until his silhouette disappeared into the night. A few moments later, the engine of his SUV kicked over. She waited, alone in the shadows, until the rumble had faded clean away. Then she dropped her head into her hands and, cringing, cursed herself for a fool.

How could she confide in a near stranger such personal information? When he'd confronted her regarding the morality of her parents' will, why hadn't she laughed it off rather than grow defensive? She knew her own mind. She did have a choice. She did.

And then…

Oh God, then there was that kiss.

The nerves that were bunched tight in her belly kicked then knotted again. She'd given herself over to the thrill of that uninvited caress so quickly and completely it frightened her— and, in some strange way, it comforted her, too. That embrace was the kind a woman would still recall in her twilight years. The kind that would cause her eyes to drift shut and chest to heave a contented sigh.

Setting off down the path bordered on either side by flowering sage, Elizabeth touched her lips, thought back on the dizzy pleasure and found she was smiling. Daniel might think he had some God-given right to force his opinion where it wasn't needed, but he still was the finest specimen of the male species she'd ever come across. Not simply because he was more attractive than most billboard models, or that he seemed to naturally dominate any space he inhabited. Despite their differences—and there were a few—she enjoyed his company. His sexy, deep laugh. It was silly, useless, and yet she couldn't help but wonder...

What if his home had been Texas or hers New York? What might have been if they'd had similar backgrounds and goals? What if, instead of apologizing for his roguish behavior, he'd hauled her back in and demanded she kiss him again?

When Elizabeth entered the house through the back patio door, she stopped dead in her tracks then let out a breath. She should have known she'd have company.

"I thought he liked my cooking," Nita said with a slight frown. The older woman held two cups in her hands.

"He said to thank you for the beautiful meal. Now, if you'll excuse me," Elizabeth said, withdrawing a pin and shaking out her hair as she headed for her room, "I'm tired."

"Good idea. I mean, will you look at the time. Past nine o'clock."

Elizabeth served Nita a fond but stern glare as she passed. "It's been a long day."

"That's all right. That's fine." Nita stared at the ceiling as if she had nothing better to do. "If you don't want to tell me what happened…"

Elizabeth held her looping stomach and groaned. "You don't want to know."

"I'm the best listener in and around these parts." With an understanding smile, she presented the cups of hot chocolate. "Made 'em when I heard his car."

Knowing when she was beaten, Elizabeth lowered herself onto a nearby settee.

She took the cup her friend offered and held the warmth between her palms. But rather than spill all about her time outside with Daniel, something even more important begged to be voiced.

"Were you surprised by my parents' will? Did Mom ever speak to you about it?"

"To my mind, it was more your dad's idea." Nita sat back and rotated the cup around in her work-worn hands. "The ranch was built up through his side of the family. Grandpa Milton was a hard man. Always talking about the responsibilities your father would need to step up and accept once he passed on. Guess your father had that in mind when he drew up that clause."

"He should have known I'd never give up the ranch. This is my home."

"You were always one to see where adventure might take you." She lifted the cup to her mouth. "Maybe things haven't changed so much."

Elizabeth knew the point Nita was making. She couldn't argue that the idea of experiencing something different and exciting had encouraged her to invite the New York architect here tonight. And, admittedly, matters had got a little out of hand when their opposing opinions had clashed and heated emotions flared.

But a kiss in the dark was far from running away and turning her back on her duty.

"I would never let my parents down," she said to herself as much as to Nita. Never.

And yet sometimes… Trying to swallow the lump caught in her throat, Elizabeth concentrated on her cup. "Do you ever wonder whether that caveat in their will was fair?"

"I don't know if that's the question you should be asking." Nita tipped forward. "Beth, you'd still have plenty to live on if you decided to walk away. One thing's a constant. Nothing ever stays the same."

"In these past years, I'd never thought beyond living here, giving it my best, making it work. One day I'd like to marry, have a family."

"I'm looking forward to it."

Elizabeth found a smile but then sobered. "Would my parents expect me to put the same ultimatum in my will?" She'd taken on the challenge to hold on to where she'd come from, who she was. But could she pass that heavy baton on to her own daughter or son? Would they hate her for it if she did?

When the lump in her throat grew all the more, Elizabeth growled at herself. "Lord, I'm all muddled tonight."

"A good-looking man will do that to you. A nice man, too, seems like. Intelligent," Nita went on, matter-of-factly. "Amusing—"

"Daniel Warren's life is in New York City," Elizabeth cut in, pushing to her feet. "Anyway, we've known each other a day."

Nita nodded as if that must be a consideration. "Do you know I was almost married?"

Elizabeth sat back down. "You never mentioned."

"I was with a bunch of girlfriends at a nightclub in Dallas, celebrating my twenty-first. He stole my heart the moment our eyes met. We danced all night and when he took me home, he cupped my cheek and kissed me. I thought I would faint for sure." Misty-eyed, Nita sighed. "I knew it would be him or no one. When he asked me to marry him two weeks later, I said yes."

Elizabeth was on the edge of her seat. "What happened?"

"He was drafted." Nita's mouth tightened and she pushed her glasses back on her nose. "Never made it home."

Her heart sinking, Elizabeth took the older woman's hand. "Oh, Nita, I'm sorry."

"Thing is, I'd rather have those two wonderful weeks than a lifetime as Mrs. Someone Else." As the faraway look evaporated, she cleared her throat and got to her slippered feet. "Best let you get to bed. Sweet dreams, Beth."

As Nita left her alone in the big room with its heavy timber furniture and portrait of Grandpa Milton hanging on the wall, Elizabeth leaned back into the cushions. The feelings Nita had for her young man must have been fierce. As fierce as the passion Daniel had coaxed from *her* tonight?

Bald truth was she wanted to see Daniel again. But given the way he'd left tonight—with an apology for weakening and kissing her when he hadn't meant to—would he want to see her?

Gnawing her lower lip, Elizabeth's frown slowly eased into a smile.

Maybe she could help him decide.

# Four

The next morning, dying for coffee, Daniel entered the Royal diner. The concierge at the hotel must have passed on the same recommendation to his crew. Rand sat in a corner booth near the jukebox, polishing off a plate of ham and eggs. As Daniel crossed over, the younger man lifted his fork in greeting.

"Hey, we missed you at dinner."

Sitting down heavily, Daniel suppressed a yawn. He hadn't slept a wink last night.

"I left a message," he said, signaling the waitress.

Grinning, Rand finished munching a mouthful of toast. "You had a better offer?"

"Something like that."

"I'm guessing from that doll in the fur."

"Her name's Elizabeth Milton."

"Whatever her name, from the look, she didn't take you back to her trailer for soda and chili dogs."

The waitress brought over a cup and poured a steamy black coffee that smelled like heaven. "What'll it be, sugar?"

"Coffee's good," he said, sliding the menu aside.

He'd been told anything ordered here was tasty and filling, but his appetite was lost, wondering what Nita had whipped up for breakfast this morning. Not to mention his obsessing about whether Elizabeth had tossed and turned all night, too.

He hadn't been able to get that confounded kiss out of his head.

Of course, that could never happen again, Daniel told himself, scalding his tongue on a long pull from his cup. He was having a hard enough time making this trip a positive experience without throwing a gorgeous heiress held to ransom by her deceased parents into the mix.

Was he ever pleased that part of his past—having no say in where he went, how long he stayed—was well behind him. After the constant struggle of being shuttled between homes, between states, no way could he tolerate Elizabeth's situation. And while nothing would change the fact that he found Miss Milton beyond attractive and interesting and charming, truth was he'd lost a little respect for her. If his parents had tried to blackmail him like that at her age, he'd have told them to go to hell in a handbag.

Rand was dabbing his mouth with a napkin. "What are you planning to do about the design?"

"Scrap it."

Reaching for his cup, Rand froze. "You mean everything?"

"You were at the meeting. The black plague was a bigger hit."

"Personally, I thought that model depicted the Old West at its best."

"Point is this isn't the Old West. Not anymore." Daniel finished his coffee and signaled for another. "Abigail's a friend but maybe I ought to retract my offer to submit."

Hell, he should be home, preparing for next month's visit from a client who needed a design for a new supermall, not downing coffee in a diner that looked like a reject from the fifties.

Leaning over the table, Rand dropped his voice. "You don't need this job, boss. Your friend will understand."

Understand? Abigail would most likely kick her heels if he suggested she might like to try someone else. The jet was fueled, ready to shoot them back to New York the moment he gave the word. Daniel took in the red-and-white upholstered booths, the diner's sleepy clientele.

What the hell was he doing wasting his time here?

Across the table, Rand nudged his chin at the entrance. "Look who just walked in."

A shiver running up his spine, Daniel spun around. Elizabeth Milton was sashaying inside like she'd been doing it all her life, which she had. Daniel told his heart to quit pounding. He didn't know how she did it, but the woman looked even hotter this morning than she had last night. A pale pink dress with a matching short-sleeved jacket and pumps that drew the eye up over the splendor of those long, shapely legs. Tiny waist. Ample bust. Every line, every crest and valley was perfection. Then there were those lips…

When a throb kicked off low in his belly, Daniel panicked and pushed to his feet. He'd pretty much made up his mind to pull up anchor. That Elizabeth Milton had strolled in now made no difference. They'd already bade each other goodbye and good luck. They had nothing more to say.

While he slapped a few bills on the table, Elizabeth stopped to speak with a woman by the counter. From her relaxed body language, it was someone she'd known a long time. Daniel shoved his wallet in his back pocket while Rand collected his laptop and sidled out of the booth, too. Elizabeth had her back to them. If he hurried, he could save them both an awkward moment and duck out before she was any the wiser.

He headed for the door, Rand hot on his heels.

"I can make myself scarce," Rand said, "if you want to, you know, say hi."

Still striding, Daniel glared over his shoulder. "We're leaving here together, packing up and saying goodbye to Royal for good."

Rand's mouth swung to one side. "You can tell Elizabeth Milton that. She's on a crash course, headed this way."

Daniel realigned his vision at the exact moment he plowed into something…someone. On reflex, his arms shot out and caught Elizabeth's upper arms as she emitted a cry of surprise and toppled backward. Daniel swore under his breath.

Idiot. He should've watched where he was going. Now, not only did he and Elizabeth have to face each other, they'd made physical contact, skin on satin skin, and that was bad news. Those big green eyes, that fresh sweet scent. If they'd been alone, he'd have gone against every scrap of common sense he possessed and kissed her again.

He made sure she was steady on her pretty pink heels then, pasting on a smile, he released his hold and dug both hands safely away into his trouser pockets.

"Elizabeth. Hey, what a surprise."

"You here trying some of our world-famous breakfast tacos?"

"Just coffee this morning."

"Pining for Nita's cooking?"

He slowly smiled. "That's probably it."

After the way they'd parted last night, why was she being so friendly? He wasn't getting even a hint of frostiness. No sign of embarrassment. In fact, she radiated confidence. It was as if that moment last night in the moonlight had never happened. She said she'd been kissed before. Maybe this kind of thing was a regular occurrence.

Rand was easing around them. "I'm off. Lots to do." He sent a smile to Elizabeth, a conspiratorial wink to Daniel, and made a beeline for the door. Daniel scowled after him. Traitor.

But if Elizabeth was big enough not to hold a grudge, considering he'd been the one to make that rash move in the first place, shouldn't he show manners enough to give her a polite moment now? Not that he intended to drag it out. He had a phone call to make. Packing to do.

So why, when he had every intention of saying, *Well, nice to have met you, have a great day,* did it come out, "Would you like a coffee?"

At his offer, barely-there dimples appeared on either side of a dazzling smile. "I'd love one."

The waitress and her coffeepot materialized beside them. "You two lovebirds need a table?"

Daniel suppressed a cough. He could take her calling him *sugar,* but *lovebirds?* Southerners were far too familiar. Talk like that could cause gossip. And gossip meant trouble.

Making certain to stand an arm's length away from Elizabeth, he indicated the booth he and Rand had shared. "I was sitting over there."

"Then let me clear those plates." The waitress walked over with them, addressing only Elizabeth when next she spoke. "Word is those pesky flamingos have ended up on your front lawn."

"I was going to make my donation today, but I thought I might keep them around a couple more days."

The woman laughed, a throaty relaxed sound. "To scare the cows?"

"Who knows?" Elizabeth said with a cheeky grin. "They might come back in fashion."

"Not where I come from," Daniel muttered, sliding into that booth.

When the waitress looked at Daniel, Elizabeth explained, "Barb, Daniel here is from New York City."

"Really? I'm hearing a lilt of an accent. South Carolina. Got an aunt from round that way."

"I call New York home now."

She deadpanned, "Whatever you say, sugar." Her focus jumped to the other side of the booth, where Elizabeth was making herself comfortable. "Can I fetch you a menu, hon?"

"Just coffee," they said together.

The waitress inspected her near-empty pot. "Need a fresh one." She headed off. "Back in a flash."

Elizabeth set her handbag down then clasped her hands on the table. "Now that we're here, I might as well go ahead and tell you the story behind the club's plaque."

If he hadn't left so abruptly, she'd have told him last night. But the situation had changed.

"No need," he said.

Her smooth brow furrowed. "Oh? Why not?"

*Because I'm throwing in my hand. Giving up and going back to where I belong.* But he didn't need to spill his guts, just because she was sitting here across from him, making him feel all jumpy, that amazing mane of hair cascading over her shoulders while she radiated curiosity and "you know you want to hold me again" vibes.

When he realized he was leaning over the table, stomach muscles clenching, he cleared his throat and lied. "A pressing matter's come up. I need to get back to the city as soon as possible."

"Nothing bad, I hope."

"Just business."

"Then I'd best not keep you."

She made to stand but instead of doing the smart thing and

letting her go, he lightly caught her hand. That same jet of sensation swam up his arm and, while he wanted to hang on, he let go fast. Physical contact was out, but now that coffee was ordered, he might as well sit back and listen.

"I really wouldn't mind hearing that story," he admitted.

She considered him for a moment before her expression eased and she lowered back down. "Well, if you have time. It goes way back to the War with Mexico. Did you notice the park next to the club headquarters?"

He got comfortable. "Sure."

"Back in the early eighteen hundreds, just beyond that park, a parcel of missionaries set themselves up. The adobe church is still there. You'd know all about those."

"Vaulted ceiling," he said. "Naves that were slightly taller than they were wide. Few windows although the light was organized to illuminate the altar to dramatic effect. The walls needed constant remudding to stand a chance against the New World elements."

She sent an impressed smile. "Ten out of ten."

Sitting back, they let Barb fill their cups before going on.

"Back in the War with Mexico," she said, when the waitress had left, "around 1846, a Texas solider found a fallen comrade. The soldier tried to save his life, but it was too late. It wasn't until he was burying the body that he came upon the jewels. A black opal, an emerald and a red diamond. The dead man had no identification so the solider decided he'd take the jewels back with him to Royal. They're so rare, each on its own is priceless, back then as well as now."

"Did anyone ever find out why the fallen soldier had them?"

"Never, which makes the legend all the more mysterious, don't you think?"

He grinned, spooning sugar into his cup. "So how do these gems relate to the plaque?"

"Apparently red diamonds are the gems of kings. That's how the first quality of the plaque came to be—leadership. The black harlequin opal is perhaps the rarest. It's said that this particular type of opal possesses healing powers and also an inner light that illuminates honesty, integrity or, more simply, justice."

"The plaque's second quality. And the emerald?" he asked, thinking of how her eyes were sparkling like priceless jewels as she spoke.

"For many centuries around the world emeralds have been thought to be the stone of peacemakers."

"Leadership, Justice and Peace." He nodded and smiled. "Nice. So where are these mysterious jewels now?"

"No one knows for sure. The story goes that the soldier had wanted sell them, buy an even bigger spread, build himself a whopping great mansion. But when he got home he struck oil."

"Black gold."

"Ended up he didn't need to sell the jewels to make it rich."

"Has anyone ever tried to find them?"

"Way back, even before Tex Langley's time—"

"The founder of the Cattleman's Club."

"That's right. A group of men got together, the legend goes, to guard the stones. Others say they were simply some of Royal's leading citizens who'd made a pact to protect the town and its citizens. There are even some disbelievers who say those men just made up the story to build their motto around."

"You don't believe that?"

Her eyes flashed. "The legend's far more exciting."

"So, if the jewels exist, where do you think they are now?"

"Somewhere safe. Not that Royal's big on crime. We're big on oil and cattle."

"There are always visitors," he said, looking at her over the rim of his cup as he sipped.

She sent him a teasing look. "Are you aiming to go treasure hunting?"

He laughed and set his cup down. "Not this visit. You look as if the thought of a treasure hunt excites you."

"I like finding new and beautiful things. A painting I can look at all day long. A song that gives me goose bumps because the words and tune are so full of meaning. Know what I mean?"

He smiled, nodded. Yeah, he knew.

"What's your favorite piece?" he asked.

"Of music?"

"Of treasure."

She stared into her cup for a long moment, considering. "I don't know that I have one." Her glittering eyes met his. "At least not yet." She tipped forward. "Do you have any hidden treasures?"

The question took him aback. He did have one. Something he rarely took out because it was that precious. It mightn't make sense to some, but the feelings it evoked...he could barely bring himself to look at it. But Elizabeth didn't need to know any of that.

"No," he lied. "I have nothing like that." Straightening, he finger combed hair fallen over his forehead. "Any more Royal stories I should hear?"

"It'd take all day to go over this town's history." She glanced at the clock above the jukebox. "And you have a flight to catch. Have you told Abigail you're leaving?"

"Not yet."

"She'll be disappointed."

*Or relieved.*

He set aside the pang of guilt and disappointment in

himself and laid another bill on the table. Glancing at his empty cup, he angled his legs out from beneath the table.

"Better get back to the hotel to pack."

"I'm headed that way. Mind if I tag along?"

He should have at least hesitated. He was leaving. No need to prolong this impromptu meeting. Get any more involved. But as he found his feet, he heard himself say, "Not at all."

That waitress stopped taking an order to watch them walk by and, it seemed, every other person they passed as they strolled down the street gave a curious smile and tip of their head. But Daniel didn't care how many tongues would wag. Soon he'd be back home where a person could truly lose himself in the rush, although he wasn't looking forward to the cooler weather, particularly after today's pleasant change. Rather than shrugging into his coat, he folded it over an arm and, with a valid reason, inspected Elizabeth's attire.

"No need for your fur today."

She flashed a cheeky smile. "It's not a real fur."

He tucked in his chin. "Not real? It looks so…"

"Expensive? It is. For a fake."

"That foxtail belt?"

"Imitation, too. One thing I did change at home was the so-called trophy room." Despite the sun, she visibly shivered. "From as far back as I can recall, I've hated the thought of those walls." She shot him a look. "Was your father into hunting?"

"He used to be." When his stomach swooped a sick loop, Daniel cleared his throat and changed tack slightly. "He's into the law now more than ever. He's a judge."

"Did he want you to study the law, too?"

"He demanded that I did." Glaring dead ahead, he set his jaw. "Only made me more determined not to."

She pretended to gape at him. "Why, Daniel Warren, you're a rebel."

"It's not rebellious to want to live your own life."

Decide when to come and when to go. He caught her downcast look. That last comment had obviously got her thinking about her own predicament, and so he swerved the conversation back onto a higher note.

"I wanted to do something different."

She nodded a greeting to a middle-aged couple walking their dachshund then asked, "What got you interested in architecture?"

"My typical male brain. I like to build things. I thought about studying to be an engineer but a friend's father was an architect. He showed me a few of his drawings one summer and I was hooked."

"So, you're a bit of an artist?"

"Couldn't paint a landscape to save my life."

"Ever tried?"

"I don't set myself up for failure." Seemed that monster steer-horn club design was an exception.

"You must have painted when you were a child," she said.

"I'm not a child anymore."

But a memory of someone else who'd loved his paint and easel at a young age pushed its way into Daniel's mind. Clenching his stomach muscles, he embraced the image for just a heartbeat then forced himself to shunt it aside. He kept walking.

"I don't paint," he said. "Never will."

"Not even to make someone you love happy?" she teased.

He answered with the utmost confidence. "Not even then."

"I've tried. Unfortunately I sucked." Something warm in his chest tugged at her soft laugh. "My dream is to one day own a Monet *Water Lilies*." A diamond bracelet glittered in the sun as she wound a long wave behind an ear. "How long have you been working for yourself?"

Daniel shook off the image of Elizabeth looking stunning, standing before a panorama of those famous flowers to reply.

"I started the company five years ago."

"From what I hear, you've certainly come a long way."

"I put in a lot of hours," he said, matching his pace to her languid stroll. "I made the right contacts and things came together."

"You work hard," she affirmed.

"Always."

"Ever give yourself time off for good behavior?"

"I treat myself when I'm on location."

"You mean when you're away from home. Like now?"

He looked at her twice. Was that a leading note to her voice, or simply wishful thinking on his part? Concentrating on the path ahead, he thought again and laughed at himself. *Get it together, Warren. The lady isn't propositioning you. She's staying true to her hospitable heritage and being polite.*

"Most of my work comes from up north or overseas," he pointed out.

"You don't get down this way often?"

"This is the first time I've been in the South in over a decade."

"Then maybe we'll bump into each other again—" she gifted him a wry smile "—in ten years or so."

The numbers tallied up in his head. In ten years he'd be forty-five. God willing, his business would still be going strong. But other than that...

Would he still have the same circle of friends? He'd probably still be a bachelor. Fact was he'd never contemplated marriage. After his abomination of an upbringing, he'd go so far as to admit he shuddered at the idea. If a woman he was seeing began to slow down whenever they passed the diamond rings laid out in a jewelry store window, he quit calling. Harsh, perhaps, but necessary. He wasn't looking for a wife. Didn't want a family or a son "to follow in my footsteps." He'd sooner put a gun to his own head.

They arrived at the hotel, the oldest and best respected in Royal, so the maître d' had told Daniel this morning on his way out. Elizabeth had stopped before a monster of a potted palm, looking like an earthbound angel as a dry breeze combed her long fair hair.

She peered up at the hotel's stone facade. "Well, this is it."

He braced his legs, shoulder-width apart. "Yes, it is."

"Good luck again." Her tone was sincere.

So was his. "You, too."

"Don't work too hard," she said over a slender shoulder as she turned and walked away.

Daniel watched as those sexy pink heels clicked a provocative tune all the way down Main's wide pavement. When she'd disappeared around the next block, he sucked down a breath and moved inside the quiet, high-ceilinged lobby then crossed the plush Oriental carpet to the lifts. In his suite two minutes later, he stopped to study his Cattleman Club's mock-up and grunted. Giant steer horns. Not one of his better ideas.

Decided, he snapped his cell phone from his belt. No use delaying.

Abigail's number was ringing when the doorbell sounded.

He tossed an impatient glance over. *Damn.* He'd meant to put out the Do Not Disturb sign. Housekeeping could make the bed after he'd vacated.

He strode over and fanned open the door. Rand stood in the corridor, surprise on his face.

"You're back already?"

Daniel huffed. "No thanks to you."

"Boss, you pay me the big bucks to read your mind. You might not have wanted me to leave but you most definitely wanted to be alone with Elizabeth Milton." Crossing his arms, he leaned up against the doorjamb. "How'd it go?"

"Actually, very well," Daniel conceded. "We had coffee. Chatted about the town's history, how that might play into a new design."

Rand straightened. "Are we back on?"

"No. We're out of here," Daniel confirmed. "Let me make a call and I'll get back to you in ten with an exit plan."

"Want me to let the pilot know?"

"Midday takeoff, if he can do it."

Rand pivoted away and had disappeared inside his own suite next door when the elevator pinged. Daniel's door was halfway shut when the earth stopped revolving and, off balance, he nearly toppled sideways.

What the devil was Elizabeth doing here?

She emerged from the elevator like a star stepping onto a red carpet. Spotting him, she bowled him over with an innocent, dimpled smile.

"Why, Daniel, you look stunned."

He remembered to breathe. To *think*.

"*Stunned* would be the word. Elizabeth, what are you doing here?"

Had Abigail sent her for some reason? No, that made no sense. Her being here didn't make sense at all.

A mysterious glint in her eye, she moved closer. "Invite me in and I'll tell you."

He got his whirling thoughts together enough to step aside and motion her in. She brushed past, that irresistible scent drifting over him, and, breathing deep, he closed the door.

"Is something wrong?"

"Depends on how you look at it."

She continued on toward the center of the room, her behind hypnotizing him as it swayed in the pale pink fitted skirt. He swallowed against a suddenly dry throat.

"I'd offer you a drink but nine a.m. seems a little early."

Pivoting around, she shrugged. "If I wanted a drink I'd have stopped at a bar."

"What *do* you want?"

"Guess there's no way around it," she said, "except to come straight out and let you know."

As she closed the distance separating them and stepped into his personal space, Daniel's respiration cranked up and sparks began to fly. When she pushed up on tiptoe, looped her arms around his neck then brought her lips to within a whisper of his, those sparks transformed into a more dangerous form of heat. Then, to really confuse him, she gifted him with a kiss that turned that heat into a world of fireworks. Compared to this, last night's experience was child's play.

As her breasts pressed in and her tongue wound out to loop sensually around his, a steamy rush of carnal pleasure swept through him, something similar to the back draft from a twenty-story fire. Hypnotized, he shaped a palm over the back of that silken hair and followed his instincts. He held her tighter, kissed her deeper and told himself to hell with consequences.

As she continued to curl around him and his every inch grew hard, Daniel couldn't stop imagining the next step. The bedroom. Clothes falling off. Urgent cathartic sex first. Long and slow and gloriously deep sex after that.

When she reluctantly pried her mouth from his, Elizabeth's breathing was ragged, too.

"I couldn't have you leave without letting you know how much I enjoyed last night."

His heartbeat booming, he stole another smoldering kiss. "Up until our discussion on family."

"That had nothing to do with us."

"I'm obviously slow, but I didn't realize there was an us."

"There can be—" she lavished a lingering kiss on the

beating hollow of his throat "—in a *here and now* kind of way."

Surging testosterone levels through the roof, he cupped her behind as she pressed against him.

"I know a man in this situation shouldn't worry about questions," he admitted as her soft, sweet lips brushed his again, "but where did this come from?"

His gut said she wasn't the type to make a habit of offering herself up on a plate like this.

"I wanted to get to know you a little better. And with you planning on leaving today, that doesn't give me much time." Her lidded eyes searched his. "If you're available, that is."

Before his mouth slanted over hers again, he growled, "Oh, I'm available."

# Five

As his lips covered hers, Elizabeth gave herself over to the heat-infused magic and let her every inhibition go. She hadn't been able to sleep last night for rehashing in her mind the roller coaster of emotions she rode whenever they'd touched. Especially when they'd *kissed*. Now Daniel knew.

She'd come here for precisely this reason.

To believe she would never feel this kind of intensity again was foolish. The world was full of attractive, interesting men. However, whether she confessed it to anyone else, she could at least admit it to herself: ten months of the year her world was limited. She could have quietly lamented Daniel Warren as a missed opportunity. But she'd decided to seize the reins and take what she wanted while she could.

Right now she wanted Daniel.

Her jacket had fallen to the floor. Zip undone, her dress was slipping past her hips, her knees. Her every nerve ending was burning, glowing white-hot. Wherever he touched, a brushfire followed.

With his mouth still covering hers, she was about to give up on unbuttoning and tear what remained of his fastened shirt wide open. Before she could, Daniel gripped her shoulders and gently eased her away. Vaguely she was aware of standing before a man she'd known mere hours wearing nothing but French white lace underwear and five-inch pink pumps. She was more concerned about why he'd broken their embrace.

She swept a fall of hair from her eyes. "Is there a problem?"

"Just thinking ahead."

When he started walking away, an alarm bell rang in her head and all the pent-up breath left her body in a whoosh. She was about to ask where he was going, why he was leaving her, when she realized and relaxed. At the door now, he was slipping the Do Not Disturb sign over the outside knob.

His shirt three-parts open, his bronzed, hard chest unashamedly on display, he slid the cell from his belt, pressed a button—presumably to switch it off—then tossed the device on the hall table before he sauntered back.

"I figure we don't want to be interrupted."

She unclasped the bra's snaps and, dropping her arms, let the cups fall.

"You figured right."

Daniel's eyes smoldered before he brought her near again. But rather than kiss her, he coaxed her around until they stood, his hard front to her back. The graze of his morning beard against the sweep of her neck sent a bevy of tingles down her entire right side while his palm, slightly rough, rode up over her quivering midriff. She sighed as the ridge of each finger one by one bumped over the sensitive tip of her breast while four hot pads slid down the front of her panties and between her thighs.

Sucking in a breath, she rolled her neck back and brought

one arm up, knotting fingers in his hair as his teeth danced across the sensitive slope that led to her shoulder.

"I'm so glad I came."

His smile tickled. "I thought I was working on that."

His thumb and forefinger came together to roll and pinch her nipple while, below, he found the part of her that already wanted to burst into flame. He drew slow, tight circles around that pulsing, smoking spot. Within seconds, her every muscle was braced, preparing for the thunderous run of contractions that crouched, waiting, a thumping heartbeat away. But then his touch moved higher. He angled her head back and his mouth claimed hers once more.

Dissolving, she let her hands slide up over the hot, smooth curve of his shoulders as he wound out of his shirt then walked her back a few paces until her calves met the seat of the couch. He was dropping kisses along her neck, over her breasts then down her ribs. As that wonderful flame inside of her leaped higher, she lifted her face to the ceiling and, quivering, hoped her knees would hold.

He slid down farther and the tip of his tongue trailed lower, too. With his help, she held on to his shoulders and stepped out of her panties. When he drew a slow line between her legs and gently parted her folds until that most private part of her was exposed, she couldn't contain a small cry of longing. His mouth covered her at the same moment he groaned with pleasure. The rumble vibrated through her blood while he flicked and swirled and then oh, so lightly nipped.

The glow of a million tiny lights quivered and swelled before, too soon, wave after breathless wave of release broke over her. Gripping his hair, she clung on to the thrill until the very last roll and he grudgingly drew away. As she buzzed and floated on the afterglow, through dreamy eyes she looked down and smiled.

She was still wearing her heels.

She swallowed her smile when she felt her weight being swept off the ground. With her safely cradled against his chest, Daniel carried her into the master bedroom.

Before he laid her on the rumbled sheets of the bed he'd slept in the previous night, he traced a line of tender kisses around her brow, her cheek and then murmured at her ear.

"You're more beautiful than I even imagined."

As she wriggled down into the cool cotton, blissfully content, he removed his shoes, the rest of his clothing and sheathed himself with a condom retrieved from his wallet. A necessity, particularly when she was unprotected. She hadn't been with a man in too long to remember.

As he came to her, she closed her eyes and relished the feel of his hard warmth wrapping around her as he gathered her near.

"No regrets?" he asked in the quiet curtain-drawn room.

Driving her palm over the powerful plateau of his chest, she assured him, "Not a one."

The white of his smile shone in the shadows before his long, strong frame covered hers. Again, Elizabeth gave herself over to the wonder of his kiss as her legs wound around the back of his rock-hard thighs and he moved, at last, entering her. A spike of pure bliss pushed from her belly all the way through to her tingling brain.

While one large palm scooped beneath to angle her hips up, his other hand curled around her head. As he moved above her, he nuzzled below her ear, growling every so often as if the feel of her surrounding him was so good it almost hurt. She removed herself from everything other than the sensation of physical abandon. When he stopped moving and his every muscle clenched and trembled above her, humming in her throat, she ran her fingertips up and down his slick sides and grazed her lips over the hot slope of his neck.

He took in a deep breath and, pushing up onto elbows,

thrust again, deeper, longer. His hot gaze locked on hers and, his forehead and chest glistening in the dim light, he ground above her. With his steely thighs bearing down, pumped biceps strained on either side of her head. He brought them both higher, feeding a fire that left her giddy and breathless.

Then his eyes squeezed shut and a rumble set off through his chest at the same time he hit an explosive spot delectably high inside of her. An all-consuming burn ripped through her body, catapulting her heart, curling her toes, at the same instant he reached that point of no return, too. As he drove in, groaned and shuddered, Elizabeth arched up to meet him.

She'd come here to claim what she could while she could.

And Daniel Warren had turned out to be far more than she'd bargained for.

# Six

Daniel was still holding on to the last of the I've-never-known-such-intensity feeling when, drawing a line down his shoulder and arm, Elizabeth asked, "Think I should take off my shoes now?"

His eyes snapped open. Thirty minutes ago he'd been ready to pack up and shove off. He'd decided Abigail and the Texas Cattleman's Club might do better without his input. Rand, as far as he knew, had advised the pilot. And yet here he was, naked in a tangle of sheets. Elizabeth Milton lay beneath him, her hair creating a soft golden frame for her glowing face, and her legs wrapped around behind his, those sexy pumps hanging off her toes.

"If wearing your heels contributed to that experience," he said, shifting to slip off one shoe then the other, "we're on to something."

After setting the pair on the floor, he scooped her close. As he searched her eyes, he wound hair behind her ear then leaned forward to tenderly kiss her lobe. At the same time, he caught the time on his wrist and frowned. Midday wasn't far enough away. Elizabeth must've been thinking the same.

Sighing, she burrowed in against his chest. "I'm going to make you late."

"You're going to make me later yet."

Cupping her jaw, he angled her face higher then kissed her again, but this time the pleasure his mouth on hers stirred was different. There was a tenderness and understanding. This morning was totally unexpected, as well as utterly off-the-charts amazing. He hoped she knew he would remember every moment...even if he couldn't stay.

As the kiss slowly broke, he wished this could be some kind of beginning rather than an end. But there was no way around the fact that he was headed out. He'd decided it was best not to pursue the Cattleman's Club project. He was done here. Elizabeth, on the other hand, was here to stay.

They lay together in the muted light, each in their own thoughts.

"Daniel, can I ask you something? Something personal."

"Sure."

"Why did you choose New York to settle down?"

His gut jumped and tightened. Yep, that was personal.

"That's a long story."

"I understand," she said in a small voice.

His stomach tightened more and, relenting, he tipped up her chin and pressed his lips to her cooling forehead. "But I'll tell you," he said, and grinned, "if you promise not to be bored."

Her expression melted and dimples appeared. "Cross my heart."

Inhaling, he thought back. Not pleasant memories, but since when could memories hurt you? People who were supposed to care for you did that.

"My parents split when I was five. My mother never got tired of telling me that my father and his family were to blame."

"That must have hurt to hear."

He huffed. *Big-time.* But as a young boy he soon developed a tactic that worked.

"After a while I stopped listening."

"Did your mother's family come from New York?"

"Connecticut. She wanted me to live up there with her. My father was adamant I would remain under his roof." Actually, it was "we." He'd had a younger brother, a friend he missed dearly. But that was something Daniel never discussed. "Given my father was a lawyer at the time, I'm stumped how he didn't win sole custody. The law isn't about justice," he told her, running a hand down her arm. "It's about who has the most money. The most clout."

"Your mother got custody?"

"It was split, straight down the middle. Half my time was spent in South Carolina in my father's empty, angry mansion, having to contend with my grandmother calling my mother a—"

His throat constricted, he cut himself off. He'd leave it to Elizabeth to fill in the blank.

"And the other half you spent up north," she said for him.

He thought back to last night at the Milton Ranch dining table. "You asked if my mother could cook."

"I remember."

"She was a health nut. Constantly lecturing about the body being your temple and pumping herself full of vitamins. When I left her home for the last time, I ate nothing but junk food for a month."

Her grin was small and sad. "How old were you when you left?"

"I was eighteen when I told them both to go to hell."

Elizabeth drew back. "Your parents?"

He lifted one shoulder, let it drop. He was sorry he'd offended her Southern sense of duty. He was sorry about a lot of things.

"By that time I'd had it up to here with being shuffled back and forth like a parcel with no voice." No feelings.

His voice had grown louder and his hands had bunched. He breathed in deeply, pushed it all out and dragged his thoughts away from incidents that couldn't be changed.

"When they both threatened to disinherit me if I didn't come around, I said I didn't want anything to do with their money. I put myself through college and the rest, as they say, is history."

"Have you seen them since?"

He set his jaw against the hollow, dark feeling rising from deep inside. "Not my father." He couldn't bring himself to speak to that egocentric, self-serving man again. "And my mother knows if she starts with telling me what's best for her boy, it'll be a long time before I darken her doorstep again."

"It makes sense now. Why you had such a strong opinion about my parents'—" she searched for a word "—requests. If my folks had behaved like that, I'm not sure I'd be falling over myself to please them, either."

Her situation was vastly different from his. "You love your ranch." She *wanted* to stay. Or at least she'd convinced herself that she did.

As if she'd read his mind and had grown uncomfortable, she sat up, hugged her sheet-covered knees and made a confession he had no trouble believing.

"I do get a little restless by the end of the ten months," she said. "I can break up the time I spend out of Royal, but I usually go through my two months away pretty well straight out the gate."

"There are no loopholes?"

"I get more time if I want to study away but there are stipulations on that, as well."

"Sounds as if they wanted their grandkids to be pure Texan."

She cut him an amused look. "I'm not thinking about having a family just yet."

*That makes two of us.*

"You'll find your own way," he assured her. Even if it turned out to be her parents' way, too.

"Do you think so?" She gave a self-deprecating smile. "I'm not sounding so sure today."

"You're young." He sat up, too, and kissed the tip of her nose. "You've got plenty of time to grow old and set in your ways."

"Like you?" she teased.

"That's right," he said, only half joking.

"Guess you've earned the right given you're, what? all of thirty-three?"

"Thirty-five."

She covered her heart and pretended to lose her breath. "If I'd known, I would never have seduced you."

His smile faded as the obvious question begged to be voiced. "Would it be impolite to ask your age?"

*Please not twenty-two.*

"I'm twenty-five."

"Don't tell me." His lips twitched. "Twenty-six next birthday." The idea of racking up another year wasn't so appealing once you hit thirty.

She narrowed her eyes, but playfully. "I know what you're thinking and ten years isn't that big of an age difference. I'm well over twenty-one."

A knot low in his gut pulled and he held that breath. They'd just made love, were sharing some secrets, but that last comment sounded a little too much like, *Where do we go from here?*

He tempered her challenging tone with a fact he'd come to appreciate more and more the older he got. "My father was ten years older than my mother."

"Sounds like they had bigger problems than a gap in birth dates."

"A lot of married couples do."

A hint of suspicion swam up in her eyes and she looked at him hard. "You're not a fan of the institution."

He leaned back against the strong timber headrest. "That's right."

Her gaze searched his until Daniel felt her unwarranted pity seep into his bones.

"Your parents failed," she murmured. "You didn't. You don't have to run all your life."

Somewhere a phone began to ring. His heart thudding, Daniel snapped a glance to his left. The bedroom extension. Five minutes ago he'd have cursed the interruption. Now? It seemed this distraction was right on time.

He picked up and blinked twice at the voice on the other end. He'd expected Rand or one of the boys.

"Daniel, is this a bad time?"

"Abigail?" He brought the sheet up higher, flicked a glance at Elizabeth. "I was going to call."

"I just wanted to let you know," Abigail said, "despite yesterday's hiccup, I have faith in you. You weren't voted American Architect of the Year for nothing. I can't wait to see what you come up with next."

Daniel was gnawing his bottom lip.

"Well, see, Abigail…that's the thing—"

"Word around town is you're seeing my friend, Elizabeth Milton," she cut in, an interested and approving note in her tone.

His smile was thin. "Nothing like a well-watered grapevine for spreading rumors." Photos would probably be in the Royal newspaper come morning.

Abigail laughed. "Anyone would think you didn't want a gorgeous, refined lady like Elizabeth Milton hanging off your arm."

He wanted to clear his throat. He'd done more than that this past hour. They'd got close enough for Elizabeth to assume she knew him, to tell him that he didn't need to keep running.

She had it wrong. He hadn't run away. When he was old enough, he'd finally stood up and pledged to do things his way and to hell with anyone who didn't like it.

But then Daniel thought about that design, Abigail's belief in him, the story behind that plaque. Mostly he thought about Elizabeth and the voice in his head telling him that, after what they'd just shared, he should do more than thank her for her time and bolt.

"When can we meet?" Abigail was asking.

"Let me get back to you, Abby. I have something to take care of."

He disconnected and, after a contemplative moment, found Elizabeth's gaze. Hugging her legs, her chin resting on her knees, she was grinning—grinning as if she could read his every thought.

"You're staying, aren't you?" she asked.

Hoping he wouldn't regret it, Daniel tipped her back onto the sheets.

"Yeah," he murmured against her lips. "I'm staying."

# Seven

The moment Elizabeth knew that Daniel wasn't on the next flight out of Royal, she was at once elated and strangely unsettled.

Her first thought was that they could share again what they had today. She'd never experienced anything like the sensations he'd stoked and coaxed from her this morning. Making love with Daniel had been an all-consuming, unprecedented lesson in mounting pleasure and rolling release. Mind, body and spirit seemed to meld until she'd felt as if she were one-half of a wondrous whole.

But as Daniel kissed her a final time then headed for the attached bath, Elizabeth bunched the sheet up under her chin and told herself to keep her head. Yes, the sex had been outstanding. Powerful. In some ways, humbling. So many would go through life without appreciating the true meaning of the phrase "making love."

But that didn't mean Daniel felt as deeply about this

morning's interaction as she did. She had no cause to think he'd told Abigail he'd stay for any reason other than the fact he wasn't ready to give up on that project. She was thankful for Abigail's sake, and for the sake of the inevitable future of the club…*if* Daniel came up with a design that captured the members' hearts and helped Abigail's push to become the establishment's first female president. The old guard would have a blue fit.

But the Texas Cattleman's Club was due for change. The club's creed—Leadership, Justice and Peace—surely applied to good women as well as good men.

Angling her legs out from beneath the covers, Elizabeth wiggled her toes into the carpet and, looking toward the bathroom door, she wondered if she ought to get dressed before Daniel returned. Probably best, she decided, collecting her shoes and padding out to the main room. She wouldn't have him think she wanted more of his time than she'd already taken.

She moved into the main room, slipped on her lingerie, her dress, jacket and finally those magic heels. And then her attention slid toward the main door and a prickle of unreality bubbled up. She didn't regret coming here, but now that she was dressed and had been left alone to wait, she found it difficult to believe that she'd actually gathered up her courage to ride that elevator up to Daniel's suite without an invitation in the first place.

Some might say she'd been reckless. Perhaps that was true. But, by God, it'd felt good to do precisely what she'd wanted, *when* she'd wanted to. She was more like Daniel than he knew.

"Was it something I said?"

At the sound of that deep, sexy voice at her back, Elizabeth spun around. Daniel stood in the doorway leading to the bedroom, a white towel lashed around his hips. A flurry of butterflies released in her stomach as she scanned the expanse of his broad chest, the muscular definition of powerful arms and super-toned abs. Her mind wound back to the way he'd held her as he'd brought them both to the brink then had flung them both over that fiery edge. She remembered the delicious thrills that had spiraled through her and, drinking in the glorious picture of him now, she only wanted to do it again.

Some men were born lovers.

His shoulder pushed off the jamb and he sauntered toward her. With every step, that pulse low inside of her beat a little deeper and each breath came a little quicker.

"You're leaving?" A line creased between his eyebrows.

With him close again, the magnet that had drawn them so fiercely together earlier began to tug again. But, although the idea was tempting, they couldn't spend all day in bed.

Could they?

Forcing her eyes from his penetrating gaze, she moved to collect her handbag where she'd dropped it in the center of the room an hour earlier.

"I should be getting on my way," she told him breezily. "You have work to do."

"Nothing that can't wait until we've enjoyed an early lunch. After just coffee this morning, I'm starved."

A saucy smile swam in his eyes as he brought her near and nuzzled the side of her neck. A jet of warmth rushed through her veins. She was helpless not to sigh and lean in more.

"Are you sure?" she murmured as his mouth traced a sensual line up to her chin.

"One hundred percent," he growled.

"You're not keen to start on your drawings?"

He tipped back to look at her sideways. "Anyone would think you're trying of get rid of me."

She laughed. *Ridiculous.* "I just wasn't expecting you to stay."

"You have somewhere else to be?"

"Not especially. Although I was going to drop by Chad's office and organize a donation so those flamingos can be on their way. I shouldn't be greedy. Someone else ought to enjoy the privilege for a while."

"Chad?" Daniel adjusted his towel. "The financial advisor who likes to keep you on his leash, that Chad?"

Her jaw set. "I explained to you—"

"Yeah. I know. He likes to look out for you."

"There's a clause in the will that dictates Chad must be my financial advisor."

"That document sure likes to dictate."

She didn't like—and didn't have to endure—the irritation darkening his face.

She collected her bag and, straightening the strap over her shoulder, she nodded toward the door. "I should go."

When she tried to skirt around him, however, Daniel reached out and caught her wrist. The disapproval burning in his eyes had turned to apology.

"Look, I'm sorry. I didn't mean to get into that again."

"That's okay. I understand."

And she did. But it was really time she left. She didn't want to regret this time and if she stayed any longer she had a feeling that she might.

Five minutes later Elizabeth stepped out of the elevator and into the hotel foyer. Although she was seen in town, in this hotel, often, she kept her head down. She didn't want to field any innocent questions about what had brought her here today.

She nodded to a stranger, sitting in a tub chair, who looked up from his newspaper and smiled. Stepping up her pace, she'd made it to the door when she ran into the one person she wasn't prepared to face.

"Elizabeth? What brings you in here today?"

*"Chad."* She tried to catch her breath and will the heat from seeping any higher up her neck. On a nervous laugh, she wet her lips and stammered some words. "I could ask the same."

"I'm here to see a client."

Now he was looking at her oddly, trying to see past the overly cheery facade.

"I was meeting a friend for lunch."

His salt-and-pepper eyebrows nudged in. "It's not even eleven."

"Thought I'd book early. You know how I like particular tables."

"Who are you meeting?"

She coughed out a short laugh. "Would you like me to hand over my appointment book?"

His eyes glinted with concern. "Elizabeth, you look shaken."

Now her face was burning. She fanned herself.

"I do feel a little piqued."

Moving to stand beside her, he rested a hand on her back. "I'll get you a glass of water."

"I'll be fine."

But he was already leading her to a comfortable settee and signaling to the concierge.

Then the situation got a thousand times worse.

Daniel stepped out of the elevator, his mind racing.

He'd rung to tell Rand that while he and the crew were free to leave today, the boss was staying. He was on his way now to the Cattleman's Club to see if he couldn't get some creative juices flowing. Somewhere the perfect idea was dying to bubble up, waiting only for the right inspiration to have it fully emerge. Thankfully, now that he'd made up his mind to step back up and face the challenge, his enthusiasm barometer had cranked up to high.

That he'd had the best sexual experience of his life this morning no doubt contributed to the energy belting through his blood. Perhaps not surprisingly, images of Elizabeth and possible club designs were converging on one another in his brain. Despite the diminished note on which she'd left, he couldn't ignore the truth. He wanted to see her again. Asking to view her house a second time would be a good excuse. But would she want to see him again? After his dig about the will, she'd practically burned rubber leaving when she had.

Daniel was striding across the long stretch of carpet when a flash of pink caught his eye and he pulled up sharply. A rush of disbelief falling through his center, he looked harder. Elizabeth had had plenty of time to leave the hotel. He wouldn't have minded bumping into her here now, except for her current company.

His lip curled.

Tremain.

But, given she'd already spotted him, there was nothing to do but stop and acknowledge them both. Then he realized Tremain was handing Elizabeth a glass of water and his insides clutched. Was she ill? And what was Mr. Have Finance Will Travel doing here anyway?

Her gaze on his, looking ashen and alarmed, Elizabeth got to her feet. And then, of course, Daniel knew. She wasn't ill but taken aback, probably at running into Tremain and then again seeing the lover she'd left moments ago.

"Daniel Warren! Seems I'm stumbling into everyone here today. Chad, you remember Mr. Warren from the club."

Tremain fairly snarled. "Yes, I remember Mr. Warren."

Again Chad Tremain didn't extend his hand. This time neither did Daniel. Then a shadow crossed Tremain's face and Daniel could barely contain a grin. He wouldn't do it to

Elizabeth, but he longed to confirm what was rattling around in Tremain's suspicious mind. *Yep, she was here to see me, chum.* Males of all species sensed competition at a hundred paces.

Not that Daniel was a long-term threat. He might not be flying home today but he would stay only as long as necessary. Elizabeth knew that as well as he knew her situation.

Daniel addressed Elizabeth in a formal tone. "Nice to see you again, Miss Milton." He noted the glass and feigned a concerned look. "You're not feeling well?"

"I was dizzy for a moment. I'm feeling much better now."

"Can I escort you anywhere?"

"No need, Warren," Tremain cut in. "I can look after Elizabeth's needs."

Daniel sent Tremain a cold look and crooked grin. "Is that right?"

Tremain looked about ready to bare his teeth when Elizabeth shoved her half-empty glass at his chest.

"Would you refill this for me, please, Chad? I'm feeling flushed again."

Tremain's stony gaze gradually left Daniel's to study Elizabeth's innocent smile. He took the glass. "Certainly."

Daniel waited until Tremain was out of earshot. "Awkward moment?"

Cutting a nervous glance around, Elizabeth tugged and straightened her jacket's hem. In a hoarse whisper, she told him, "There's no need for Chad to know what happened this morning."

"I'd have no trouble informing him."

Her eyes widened at his gravelly tone and she whispered again, sterner this time, "Don't you dare stir up trouble."

"On one condition."

Striking a pose, she folded her arms. "Are you proposing blackmail?"

He wondered if he saw a touch of excitement light in her eyes.

"Nothing quite so dramatic. I'd like to visit the Milton Ranch again."

She gaped at him for five full seconds before a smile flirted with one side of her mouth. "I'm sure Nita would love to accommodate you. I warn you, though. This time you'd better stay for dessert."

"You can bet on it," Daniel said.

"Can bet on what?"

Daniel flicked a glance to his left. Tremain was back. And while Daniel appreciated Elizabeth's position with regard to privacy, he wasn't about to hide behind corners like a kid. Elizabeth was woman enough for Tremain to hear at least part of the truth.

"I invited myself over to Milton Ranch for supper."

Gaze firing, Tremain actually squared up. "Rather presumptuous of you, isn't it, Warren?"

Daniel shrugged. "We Northerners are known for it."

Chad's shoulders went back at the same time Elizabeth stepped between them.

"Chad, did I mention I'm desperate to get those plastic flamingos off my lawn? Could we organize a donation today?"

Tremain's glare slid away from Daniel, who hadn't had this much fun since he'd whipped the butt of a college rival at tennis. It felt good to win.

Tremain addressed Elizabeth. "I can organize that for you, Elizabeth, although we'll need to discuss an amount."

"Do you have time to sit down now?" she asked.

Tremain eyed Daniel again before extending his arm for Elizabeth. But she either didn't see the gesture or ignored it.

Daniel grinned to himself. *Suck on that, Tremain.*

Before moving off, she offered her hand to Daniel. "I'll see you this evening."

"Let's say, seven?"

As their hands met and squeezed, a smile twinkled in her eyes. "Seven sounds just fine."

Daniel was tempted to watch as she moved off, but to be on his way was probably wiser. He'd riled Tremain enough for one day. He asked the doorman to have his rental brought up and soon he arrived at the Texas Cattleman's Club.

Alighting from the vehicle, he surveyed the club's grounds. Manicured gardens and lawn were set amid majestic sprawling plains dotted with small trees, which were bowed by prevailing southern winds. His attention veered toward the club building, grand, solid and appropriate...but also, to his taste, due for at least a good brushup.

Because of the sheer size of the state, its variations in weather and scattered patterns of settlement, Texas architecture enjoyed a diversity of styles. The clubhouse was a mixture of Victorian—red granite and timber exterior, sandstone and elaborate carved woodwork interior—and Spanish Colonial, an ancestor of the ranch-style house—thick stuccoed walls and small windows that invited in the breeze and kept out the heat. The structure conveyed a sense of strength. Endurance. And that was key.

So how to keep the heart of this club while promoting the new twenty-first-century feel Abigail and her supporters were after?

Daniel was wandering around a far corner of the building when he heard a hushed but intense conversation in progress. Male voices...the words "baby" and "blackmail." Three men came into view, huddled together beneath a giant oak. Not wanting to intrude, he was pivoting away when one of the men glanced over then all three stopped to glare.

The nearest, a tall man with brown hair and hawkish hazel eyes, edged around to face him. "Can I help you?"

Daniel held up a friendly hand. "Just taking a stroll of the grounds. Admiring the club." When their stares intensified, he added, "The name's Daniel Warren."

That same man's eyes flashed. "Abigail's star-chitect."

And then it clicked and Daniel straightened his spine. "And you must be Bradford Price."

This was the man who was running for presidency of the club and Abigail Langley's nemesis. No wonder he was looking at Daniel as if he wanted to grab him by the collar and personally escort him off the grounds. And what was that about blackmail? Such murmurings didn't bode well for a club whose motto was Leadership, Justice and Peace.

"I'm Abigail's guest here, yes." Daniel jerked a thumb over his shoulder. "I'll be on my way. Let you all get back to your conversation."

As he rotated away, Daniel saw in Brad Price's eyes that he wondered how much of the conversation the outsider had heard. Enough to be suspicious, that's how much. But not enough to want to dig any further. Seemed there was a whole lot more going on in Royal than an unprecedented election.

As she and Chad took a seat in a private corner of the hotel, Elizabeth got straight to business and mentioned the amount she was more than comfortable with donating to the Helping Hands Shelter in exchange for having the flamingos removed.

Sitting back, Chad slowly shook his head. "You don't need to donate that much."

She frowned. "It's a wonderful cause." One of the best, to Elizabeth's mind. Although she kept it quiet, she'd been helping out individual families for a while now. "That women's shelter has helped a lot of people in need, children included. It offers a wonderful service for the community."

"No doubt. And it's great to have such a generous spirit. You never tire of giving. But, Elizabeth, you don't need to go overboard."

She eyed the man who had been directing her finances— her life—since her parents' deaths, and a sick, empty feeling caved in around her. She'd told Daniel she wasn't a child, but the truth was Chadwick Tremain made her feel like a minor. A mere girl with no rights. She was a twenty-five-year-old woman with a sharp mind. A mind of her own.

Chad didn't think she needed to "go overboard."

She clasped her hands on the table before her. "Kindly have your office transfer the amount I've stipulated into the shelter's account today."

"Elizabeth, I'm telling you in my professional opinion—"

"And I'm telling you that you are my advisor, not my keeper."

"Your father wanted your affairs looked after."

"I can look after my own affairs."

"In the will—"

Her fist thumped on the wood. "I'm sick of hearing about that will!"

Chad's head snapped back. For a moment, Elizabeth thought he might raise his voice at her. But then he skipped a glance around the room and saw that no one was near enough to notice her outburst. He smoothed the line of his royal-blue tie, the one with which he always wore his diamond pin.

She'd never liked that tie.

"I should be on my way." She stood.

So did Chad. "I wish you wouldn't leave like this."

She stopped, remembered how fond her father had been of this man and pulled in a leveling breath.

"I'm not ungrateful for your help—"

"That's what I'm here for."

"But I don't need your help." When his face fell like a boy who'd been told his dog had run away, she softened the blow. "Or not as much as I may have in the past." She thought of eighteen-year-old Daniel standing up to his parents and cutting his ties, and she lifted her chin.

"Make that transfer, please, Chad."

As she walked out and onto Main, Elizabeth clasped her hands at her chest. Still she couldn't stop them shaking. She'd never felt so energized. So on edge. She'd accepted her lot with regard to the ranch. Had embraced it. Why had Daniel Warren come along and turned everything upside down?

# Eight

## Underline

"We're having a guest again tonight," Elizabeth announced to Nita as she entered the Milton Ranch kitchen on the way through to her room.

Nita set down her chopping knife and followed Elizabeth down the main hall and up the stairs. "Anyone I know?"

Grinning, Elizabeth shrugged out of her jacket. "Yes, Nita. It's Daniel Warren."

"I'm glad to hear you sorted out your differences."

In her bedroom, Elizabeth reached behind and unzipped her dress, remembering this morning when she'd arrived at his hotel suite door and found the courage to let him know how she'd felt. Now that time spent in Daniel's arms, in his bed, seemed like some wild fantasy. A dream. She could easily believe she'd imagined the whole amazing interlude except for the tingling afterglow still warming her skin and the fact they were seeing each other again tonight. She wasn't one to look a gift horse in the mouth. She had every intention of repeating the experience.

As far as having sorted out their differences…

"Let's say," Elizabeth said, slipping off her shoes, "we've come to an understanding."

"Glad to hear it. I'll let my mother know I'll be over tomorrow instead."

An earlier conversation flashed to mind and Elizabeth wheeled around from her set of drawers. "Nita, I completely forgot."

Mrs. Ramirez lived in the next town. The following day was the anniversary of her husband's death, Nita's father. Nita liked to keep her mother company and stay overnight.

But Nita was shaking it off. "I'll go tomorrow. I'll be there early."

Elizabeth dug some riding breeches from a drawer. "Don't you dare change your plans."

"You're not going to *cook*." Slipping a polishing rag from her pocket, Nita rubbed over the oak dresser. "You don't want to frighten the boy off. Then again, your mother couldn't flip an egg. Didn't stop your dad from proposing."

Pulling on the breeches, Elizabeth paused to give the older woman a pointed look. "Nita, I'm not marrying Daniel Warren."

"Did I say that you were?"

Nita concentrated on polishing the same spot on the dresser while Elizabeth, shaking her head fondly, shimmied into a checked shirt then dropped onto the edge of the bed, socks in hand. She was feeling restless, to say the least. The best way to work off energy was to jump in a saddle and charge off for a long, hard ride over the plains.

Her father had taught her to ride. Even how to rope on horseback. Although he'd denied it, Elizabeth knew her dad was disappointed he hadn't had a son, particularly when she'd begun to show more than an interest in doing her nails and face and hair. Then came her unquenchable curiosity in all things outside of the Lone Star State. Although contained now, that curiosity hadn't waned.

Nita moved on to polishing the bed headboard. "Why don't you take him to Claire's?"

Finished slipping on her socks, Elizabeth pushed to her feet. "Good idea."

Intimate atmosphere, scrumptious cuisine, Claire's was the finest restaurant in Royal. This evening the usual Friday night regulars would be there, Chad included.

Elizabeth's mouth twisted to one side.

Maybe she ought to reconsider defrosting some ribs and firing up the grill.

"Is there anything you need before I head off?" Nita had moved to hang Elizabeth's jacket.

"I'll be fine." She dropped a kiss on Nita's cheek and gave her arm a squeeze. "Give my best to your mom."

"Don't forget that dessert's in the fridge if Daniel wants a slice."

"Enough with the organizing." Elizabeth playfully shepherded Nita out her door. *"Go."*

As Nita moved down the hall, Elizabeth thought she heard a car. She moved to a window. No visitors but the flamingos caught her eye. Before heading out for her ride, she'd make sure Chad had organized the payment for the shelter.

She lowered into the chair set before her desk and laptop, brought up her email account and smiled. A message from Chad, brief, formal. He'd transferred the money to the shelter and for the amount she'd requested.

Elizabeth mentally punched the air.

*Score one for the kid.*

As she shut down the browser, the screen saver appeared, a picture of a hauntingly beautiful Scottish castle she'd visited one vacation. She wanted to see Australia next, but needed more time if she was going to see everything in one trip. She had to experience snorkeling over a coral shelf in the Great Barrier Reef. Climbing the Sydney Harbour Bridge, overlooking stretched blue silk waters and the enormous sails of the Opera House, was a must. No way would she miss visiting the Red Centre, watching the sun set over massive Uluru and absorbing a masterpiece created from God's personal palette.

And there was so much more.

The generations-old hall clock struck the first of twelve. Elizabeth blinked back to reality and held the empty feeling that suddenly invaded her stomach.

Her mother had introduced her to the travel bug when they'd suggested boarding school in Europe. Neither of her parents had traveled extensively, but her mother, particularly, had wanted her daughter to grow up with a keen sense of culture and class. Sometimes Elizabeth wondered if they should have done her a favor by keeping her sojourns confined to within Texas, or at least the States. If she'd never known what amazing experiences and sights were out there, she wouldn't miss it so much now.

Wistful, she pushed back her chair and meandered down the hallway, down the stairs, past that clock, the media room and the library, the area which had previously been her father's trophy room. Every nook and cranny lived, embedded in her brain, as clearly as the computer had stored that remarkable shot of Scotland. No denying, she felt comfortable here. *This* was home.

How would she feel, how would she cope, if she ever decided to ignore the clause in her parents' will and simply fly away?

When Elizabeth arrived at the kitchen, tonight's dinner with Daniel came to mind again. She wouldn't try to cook.

In France she'd taken lessons in cuisine preparation, but, frankly, while she adored the flavors and textures, whipping up fabulous dishes didn't come easily. She truly admired people like Nita who effortlessly created mouthwatering meals.

She dialed the Royal Hotel to pass on the change of plans. When the receptionist answered, Elizabeth gave her name and asked to leave a message for Daniel Warren, but at that moment, the receptionist told her that Daniel had walked into the hotel lobby. A few knocking heartbeats later, Elizabeth heard his deep, sexy voice on the line.

"I hope you're not going to renege on our arrangement tonight," he said.

His tone was teasing, but also curious. Did he honestly think she'd cancel?

"Nita won't be home tonight. And I need to be up-front and say my attempt at barbecue leaves a lot to be desired."

"Can you suggest a place? Snails don't need to be on the menu."

She laughed. "We'll save that for France."

The sentiment was an innocent one but once it was out, a shard of panic dropped through to her toes. It sounded as if she were inviting him to Paris. With almost all of her two months vacation time this year gone, she couldn't and *wouldn't*. Although the idea certainly had its merits.

She brushed over the gaffe.

"I can recommend Claire's. It's an upscale place that serves delicious food."

"I'll make the reservation and collect you at seven. And, Elizabeth?"

"Hmm?"

"If you want me to last through dinner, show some mercy and don't wear those heels."

* * *

Smiling, Daniel reluctantly hung up from the sound of Elizabeth's laughter. Crazy but he'd missed it more than he'd realized.

While he'd inspected the club earlier he'd kept his mind on the job, working through new ideas. But now that he was back in this environment, the memories of his and Elizabeth's time spent filtered back. The scent of her, the silken heart-thumping feel. He'd been with women before—plenty. But there was something truly unique, and inspiring, about Elizabeth Milton. Something he couldn't get enough of. That what they shared was purely "here and now" made its promise all the more appealing.

Standing at the far end of the polished timber counter, he motioned to catch the receptionist's eye. He wanted to know if Rand had checked out yet. But it seemed the woman was engaged in what was fast becoming a heated conversation with someone else. He didn't want to eavesdrop but he couldn't ignore the spat, particularly when it centered on Abigail Langley and her push for the club's presidency.

"We women have no right shoving our noses in their business," the second woman with a helmet of light purple hair was saying.

"You're entitled to your opinion, Addison." The receptionist nudged her chin higher. "And I'm entitled to mine. Men don't have dibs on leadership. Not anymore. There's a lot of us who feel the same way."

"You know she wants to tear down the club," Addison said, "and start again, like suddenly that century-old building's not worth a dime."

The receptionist flicked an uncomfortable glance Daniel's way and lowered her voice. "We have company. This isn't the place."

The other woman shifted her focus then her gaze sharpened. "You're that architect she brought down." Her eyes narrowed. "We don't want your kind here. Go home."

"Boss, everything all right?"

Taken aback, Daniel rotated to find Rand, standing at his back, jaw set, ready to do whatever needed to be done. The woman named Addison looked big enough, and angry enough, to ram a steer.

"Everything's fine."

Rand followed as his boss crossed to a settee. "Sounds like the natives are growing restless."

"Local politics aren't my concern."

"Not unless you get lynched."

"The Civil War's over, remember?"

"Tell Mrs. Robert E. Lee over there that."

Daniel stifled a chuckle. Matters surrounding elections often drove high feelings. He wished Abigail all the best with her efforts to infiltrate this previously held man's domain. Other than that, he wasn't interested. Wouldn't get involved.

Daniel nodded at the laptop case Rand carried.

"You heading off?"

Rand nodded. "Sure you want to stay?"

"I have a job to do."

"And a certain lady to see?"

Daniel opened his mouth to deny it, but what was the point. "As a matter of fact, yes. I'm taking Elizabeth Milton to dinner this evening."

"She must be special."

"I'm not staying because of Elizabeth."

"It's none of my business, boss."

"Then why are you grinning?"

"Was I grinning?"

He knew damn well he was and, for a moment, Daniel thought Rand had somehow learned about his and Elizabeth's escapade this morning. But that wasn't possible, even if Chadwick Tremain obviously had his well-founded suspicions.

Daniel shook his second-in-charge's hand and moved off toward the lifts. "I'll see you when I get back."

Rand reminded him. "Be careful not to overstay your welcome."

When Daniel received a message from Elizabeth saying she'd meet him at the restaurant, he wondered why she wouldn't want him to collect her.

Where women were concerned he was the old-fashioned type. A man should collect a lady, be on time, open her door. He couldn't say he'd slept with a woman he'd known less than twenty-four hours before. To balance that anomaly, he couldn't remember wanting to enjoy that time again so much.

Perhaps she'd planned to already be out and about, he decided, nodding to the doorman as he entered Claire's Restaurant that evening. And if Elizabeth had her own transportation, was he still on for looking over more of her home later this evening, or was she planning on saying good-night here?

Daniel rubbed the back of his neck.

After being so forthright this morning, would she play hard to get now?

But then, as the maître d' inquired about a reservation, Daniel saw her, dressed in a red satin cocktail number, alone in a secluded corner. Her hair was down, flowing around her shoulders and back like a silken river. She sat as poised as a princess, but he knew firsthand she possessed the spirit of a tiger. With his gaze combing her arms and legs, Daniel's blood stirred and heated. Damn, he'd forgotten just how gorgeous she was.

Noting she hadn't seen him arrive, he thanked the maître d' and sauntered over. Perhaps he should wind around and up behind then surprise her by planting a hot kiss on one side of her neck. But could he stop at one?

He set off, weaving around tables dotted with patrons involved in private conversations or perusing menus. He was only a few strides away from reaching her table when he recognized a voice and an unsettling feeling gripped his middle. After this morning, he'd know that drawl anywhere.

Bradford Price.

Daniel glanced to his right. Sure enough, Brad Price was seated with a number of others. His expression was open, confident, unlike earlier today when he'd been agitated about babies and blackmail. Daniel wondered what Brad's supporters would say if they knew their candidate to head the renowned Cattleman's Club was likely knee-deep in scandal involving blackmail.

Price's focus snaked over Daniel's way. With a steely gaze, Price sent a halfhearted salute. Daniel tipped his head in response. Good luck in trying to keep a secret that big in such a small town, Daniel thought.

When he reached Elizabeth's table, he found her frowning, her gaze shifting between Price and him.

"You know Bradford?" she asked.

"I know of him."

Tipping close, Daniel grazed his lips over her temple. His lungs absorbed her sweet scent and recollections of their time together in his suite this morning flooded his senses. It was on the tip of his tongue to suggest they eat later. He was hungry, but he was hungrier for her. Then Brad Price's cocky laugh filtered across the room. Daniel was brought back and he straightened to his full height.

"This is obviously *the* place to dine in Royal." He took his seat. "Should we expect Mr. Tremain, too?"

"Chad?" She wound a wave of blond hair away from her cheek and shrugged. "Possibly."

"There goes the appetite," he muttered, shaking out his napkin.

"He's not that bad." She settled back in her chair, looking a little smug. "He made that donation today. I'll be flamingo free come morning."

"*You* made the donation, Elizabeth. Don't forget Tremain works for you. He needs to be reminded of that more often, too."

"If you're uncomfortable, we can leave."

He took in her stiff expression, her suddenly tight tone, and kicked himself. They were here to enjoy each other's company, some good food, not to rehash a situation that he had no power over and no right to interfere with.

He cleared his mind.

"No. This is good." He signaled for the waitress. "Did you drive yourself here?"

"Abigail wanted to meet for a drink and discuss some campaign plans. She dropped by the ranch to pick me up."

"You should have asked her to join us."

"She didn't want to be a fifth wheel. And she said she'd had a big day." She angled her head and those glossy full lips gleamed in the candlelight. "How did you occupy yourself this afternoon?"

"I dropped by the club again."

"Any ideas?"

"Nothing that blew me away."

Unlike that tiff when he returned to the hotel. Despite the cool act in front of Rand, the interaction had surprised and unsettled him. He'd vowed to put it out of his head but now he was interested to know.

"There was a guest today at the hotel's reception," he said. "She was very vocal about the fact that nothing about the club should be changed. She made it clear she didn't want the leadership to pass into the hands of anyone other than a cattle*man*."

"A woman said that?" He nodded. Elizabeth's lips tightened as she cast a glance around the candlelit tables. "There's all kinds of dynamics involved. That woman's entitled to her opinion."

"That's what the hotel receptionist said. People might like progress," he grunted, "but tradition dies hard."

Elizabeth knew that as well as anyone. She was legally *chained* to it. But he wouldn't get into that again, either. They were talking about the club and the coming election.

"Between you and me," he asked in a subdued voice, "do you think Abigail's wasting her time running? Brad Price seems like a snaky son of a gun."

"Or, do you want to know if I think she's wasting *your* time?"

A corner of Daniel's mouth curved up. "Either way," he said, "I'm not sorry I accepted her invitation to come to Royal."

He was about to tell Elizabeth again how pleased he was that she'd shown up on his doorstep unannounced this morning. That he was beyond happy she'd agreed to see him again tonight. But his cell phone rang before he had the chance.

"Sorry." He grabbed the phone off his belt and muted the sound.

"Don't you want to know who it is?"

"Later. Right now I'm having dinner with one of the Lone Star State's most interesting and, might I say, beautiful women."

Pretending to be coy, she tucked in her chin. "You might live in New York but your silver tongue is pure South."

When the waitress arrived, Daniel ordered wine and the specialty of the house—pepper filet mignon with whiskey sauce. Elizabeth went with what she said was her favorite, chicken-fried steak with greens.

His eyebrows shot up. The contradictions kept coming. "From escargot to chicken-fried steak?"

"I grew up on the stuff." She reached for her water glass. "What do they eat in South Carolina?"

"I remember a lot of shrimp, grits and fried cabbage." Other memories surfaced—unpleasant ones—and he cleared his throat. "Course, that was a long time ago."

She nodded slowly, tried to smile.

"Has your dad ever tried to get in contact?" she finally asked.

"Not for a while now."

Her glistening gaze held for a long moment then fell away. "Strange how things work out. I'd do anything to be able to see my father again. Mom, too."

Daniel groaned. Life wasn't always fair. He might not agree with the clause her parents had included in the will but that didn't mean she didn't love them and wished they were still around. Years ago he'd wished for miracles, too.

Approving the wine sample the waiter poured, he set down his glass. "You must have a lot of great memories."

"All around. Every day." Elbows on table, she rested her chin in the vee of her palms. "My best memories are around family occasions. Thanksgiving. Christmas. They always did something special for birthdays."

He nodded, letting the waiter know to fill both glasses while mouthwatering aromas and the sound of clinking silverware filtered through the room. "Special like what?"

"For my thirteenth birthday, my father put on our own rodeo at Milton Ranch. There was entertainment and prizes. People came from miles around."

Bucking broncos, barrel racing, scrambling rodeo clowns. He gave a crooked smile. "Sounds like fun."

"I had my first kiss that day. A boy I'd crushed on for months. He was leaving with his folks the next week for California."

"First kiss, huh?" He tried to think but his own was too far back to remember.

"As our lips—or should I say *braces*—met, he backed me up against the rough fence rails. Unfortunately a whole pile of livestock had been there before us." Her nose scrunched. "We were wearing boots but still not good."

He chuckled. "Amazing you weren't scarred for life."

"He said he'd write. He did once. Even sent a silver locket in the envelope. Sometimes I wonder whatever happened to Dwight Jackson."

He couldn't tell if the faraway look that had come to her eyes was feigned or sincere.

"If I didn't know better I'd think you were trying to make me jealous."

One teasing eyebrow arched. "Are you?"

"To my core."

Growling playfully, he leaned forward. Their mouths touched over the center of the table and that same delicious got-to-have-you feeling scorched his every nerve ending. The temptation to slide his hand around her nape and deepen the kiss was almost too great to resist. But, given their current environment, unfortunately, that wasn't an option.

Soon their meals arrived. The filet mignon was sublime, Elizabeth enjoyed her chicken-fried steak, and the next hour evaporated as they talked over the candlelight, first about Nita being out of town tonight, then the places they'd visited around the world and spots they still wanted to see.

As they finished the last of the wine, the waitress appeared and Daniel looked around. The restaurant crowd was thinning.

"Can I interest you in dessert?" the waitress asked.

Elizabeth leaned closer to Daniel. "Nita wanted me to let you know that caramel apple cheesecake is still fresh."

Looking up, he handed the waitress back her menu. "There's your answer."

And his. He'd wondered if, after giving so generously of her time this morning, she might make him suffer and string him out. But from the inviting smile simmering in her eyes now, hopefully she'd want him to stay for breakfast, too.

As they moved away from the table, Daniel noticed Bradford Price had left and his mind clicked over. Did Abigail know anything about the hushed conversation he'd overheard? *Blackmail* was an ugly word that accompanied an ugly deed, particularly when you were standing for office, public or private.

"What's the story behind Mr. Price?"

"Bradford's an extremely successful businessman. And playboy. His family's in banking. They founded most of the artistic foundations in Houston and Dallas. He has a solid reputation but when Abigail first threw her hat into the election ring, he made jokes behind her back. Their rivalry since high school is a bit of a legend in these parts."

He pulled a pained face. "I do like my anonymous life."

"I hear you're nothing less than a celebrity in your profession," she retorted, grinning. "I'm sure you don't lead a sheltered life, Daniel."

"No. But I try not to attract unwanted attention."

"Trouble sometimes follows when you deal with family, friends, community."

He looked at her twice and knew, despite her angelic expression, she was having a dig at him. But, right or wrong, he was too old to change. He might live a busy life but it wasn't cluttered with family baggage. Not anymore.

They drove to Milton Ranch, Daniel tossing around some ideas on the new clubhouse design. He spoke with Elizabeth about the history of architecture in the region, from Spanish Colonial and Mexican Republic through to Modern and beyond.

"Do you think there's a possibility in reinventing any of those for the design?" she asked.

"In my opinion, I think we need something totally new." He grinned. "Easier said than done."

"Perhaps that cheesecake will help."

Her hand found his thigh and, in that instant, nothing mattered but the wash of warmth the contact inspired. He'd come up with something that would grab the hearts of the Cattleman's Club members. But tonight he was more interested in Elizabeth's heart.

When he steered the vehicle up before the house, the arcing beam from headlights let them know they still had company—the flamingos. Daniel dropped the gear into Park.

"Maybe you should drum up an army of gnomes to keep them company."

"And we could stick plastic primroses in their little pots." Opening his door, he froze and she laughed. "Daniel, I was joking."

He accompanied her up the path and waited while she unlocked the tall timber front door, all the while trying to rein in the heightened awareness tugging at his senses…the anticipation of gathering her close and claiming her mouth with his. Rocking back on his heels, he inhaled the perfume of fall wildflowers and told himself to be patient. Good things came to those who waited.

"Why don't I cut you a slice of cake," she said, setting her keys on the hall stand, "and we can take a tour."

"Sounds like a plan."

She walked a couple of feet ahead, showing him the way down a long, high-ceilinged hall decorated in timber panels and the occasional painting depicting the area, glorifying the cowboy legend with lassos and dust flying. Daniel imagined the smell of cattle and dogwood blossoms, the magic of a Texas sunset and stories of cattle rustling told over campfires.

In the kitchen, Elizabeth extracted a cream-topped pie from a monster refrigerator and Daniel's taste buds tingled. He wished he'd left more room.

"Are you joining me?" he asked.

"If I consumed all the desserts Nita has prepared over the years, I'd be the size of our barn." Crossing back from a cupboard, plates in hand, she winked. "But tonight's special."

Daniel wet his lips. *Yes, it is.*

When the pie was cut and waiting in individual bowls, Elizabeth slapped a spoon in his palm and, with a lift of her chin, indicated he should follow. Side by side, sampling their first creamy taste of pie, they traversed that hall again, this time ducking into a massive double-story ceilinged room, housing studded maroon leather chairs and walls of books. With the lingering aroma of pipe smoke hiding behind heavy baroque curtains, Daniel surveyed the sea of polished timber floor, numerous ornate architraves and a padded window seat, which looked out over green patches of lawn. He crossed to a section of old spines and eased out one musty book.

"*Beyond Good and Evil* by Friedrich Nietzsche." Impressed, he set down his bowl and carefully opened the hardback cover. "Your father enjoyed a little light reading."

"That book belonged to my mother. Dad was more a *Billy the Kid* fan."

He shot her a look. "Your mother read this?"

"Sure. When I was old enough she passed it on to me." Her eyes lit. "Have you read Nietzsche?"

Heavy-duty philosophy?

"My reading material comprises titles like *Architectural Digest*." Sauntering close again, he sent her an intrigued grin. "Just how many layers do you have?"

"You mean in general," she said as she dropped a look down over her red silk dress, "or just tonight?" She slid a spoonful of pie into her mouth and sashayed out the room.

After loosening his tie, Daniel collected his bowl and followed.

"This is the nine-ball room," she said, a few moments later.

Daniel examined the full-size table, the timber-and-steel-studded bar and, most impressive, a ceiling fresco portraying a stampede of wild horses. Nice.

Next she introduced him to the sitting room, the media room, an amazing A-framed undercover outdoor area…in all he guessed around 20,000 square feet of luxury. Every room boasted stylish symmetry that would be bathed in natural light during the day, some with crossbeam ceilings and murals. Numerous wood-burning fireplaces, granite floors in wet areas… Daniel had a better idea of why Mr. Milton wanted to keep it in the family.

But on a professional note, nothing jumped out and said, with regard to the Cattleman's Club, *Hey, run with this!*

They'd climbed an elegant staircase to the second story, where the majority of bedrooms where located, he presumed, thumbing a smear of cream from his lower lip into his mouth. As if reading his mind, she crossed through an opened double doorway, clicked on some muted down-lights and moved into a room decorated completely in snow-white and the exact green of her eyes.

"Now this is my suite. Here's the fireplace," Elizabeth said, gliding with catlike grace over the spongy carpet. "My private retreat." She indicated a silk-covered chaise, facing a window that overlooked the lit waters of an Olympic-size swimming pool. "That way to the attached bath," she said, and gestured to the left, "and this is where I like to do the majority of my sleeping."

In a sensual, fluid move, she lowered herself onto the edge

of a king-size bed, which was covered with a plump white duvet.

His pulse booming, he started forward as she slipped off her sexy red heels. When he joined her, she was reaching behind, removing the heavy ruby necklace that graced the slim column of her throat. An heirloom, perhaps.

"And that concludes the tour," she told him, setting the necklace on the duvet and curling her legs up to one side. Her gaze meshed with his, she languidly rolled back and sank into airy white. "I think you've seen enough tonight."

His gaze devoured her lips. "Not nearly enough."

He slid off his tie and released his belt, all the while drinking in the alluring sight splayed out before him. When she stretched out, telling him without words to hurry and join her, he finished unbuttoning his shirt but then dropped to his knees. Collecting her foot, he brushed his lips up and down the bare instep. Her toenails were painted to match her dress. Was her lingerie the same shade? A rich, sexy red.

His palms slid up her smooth shins, knees, before he dropped a slow, moist kiss on her thigh. Her head rolling to one side, she sighed as his fingers filed up beneath her dress and twined around thin silk bands sitting high on each hip. When she arched, helping, he peeled the scrap of fabric down and off her legs. He wound out of his shirt then began a mouth-to-skin glide up the inside of one leg until he reached the point where he was gripping red satin and dragging it higher.

The tip of his tongue slid up between her thighs, delaying long enough to circle and tease her swollen nub, which made the cradle of her hips twist, dip and lift. After a gentle nip, he moved to capture her hem and ease the dress up over her waist, her breasts. When she lay naked on the bed beneath him, her hair fanned out and eyes heavy with want, he shifted back to remove his trousers.

Daniel had seen Elizabeth without clothes this morning, but as he gazed on in the soft light now her curves sent his erection into a near spasm. Controlling the urge to drive her thighs apart and take her quickly, he flipped back the duvet and joined her as she wiggled up then under the cover.

Lying front to front, the tips of her breasts teasing his chest, she coiled an arm around his neck and asked, "Do you have anywhere to be tomorrow?"

He nipped her lower lip and groaned as a spike of pleasure speared through him. "Only here with you."

Humming against his lips, she murmured, "Mr. Warren, you read my mind."

He made love with an agonizing lack of speed, firstly tasting the line of her collarbone while lightly pinching and rolling the tips of each breast until she begged him to take her into his mouth. As he lowered and captured one rosy tip, Daniel recalled this morning—forbidden, fun and over way too fast. Tonight's union would be about exploring places Elizabeth had never been before, had never known existed. He planned to take them both to heights filled only with bone-melting sensation and incandescent light.

He moved higher, his mouth searching out hers again, probing and teasing while his hips against hers mimicked the slow, stoking rhythm. When her lips left off savoring his and began to trail down his chin, over the pulse beating wildly in his throat, Daniel lay back, resting a forearm over his eyes and warning himself to hang on.

She slid farther down, all the way, until she reached his hard, ready length. As her mouth slipped over the head of his erection and her tongue swirled a lazy loop again and again, he groaned and, stemming the thundering force shooting through his veins, made a this-is-way-too-good fist.

Cupping him with one hand, dragging and squeezing with the other, she accepted more and more of him. The suction growing, his energy swelling, Daniel held tight every muscle as he moved in time and stroked her hair. At the same moment perspiration broke on his forehead, one dainty hand splayed up over his quivering belly, driving higher to rub one side of his chest then the other. Each time her palm grazed a nipple, a line directly connected to his manhood vibrated then tugged. When her teeth got involved, grazing skillfully up and down, on the brink, Daniel grabbed her shoulders and hauled her up.

Surprised, she threw hair back from her face. "I wasn't finished."

"I nearly was."

A wicked gleam swam up in her eyes and she shifted until she straddled him, a knee on either side of his hips, her parted thighs hovering over his engorged glistening length. Setting her palms side by side on his ribs, she tipped forward and stole a heart-hammering kiss that set a sky of fireworks shooting off in his head.

With her breasts brushing his chest, she kissed him until he didn't know which way was up. With each passing second he only knew he wanted to feel her velvety warmth wrapped moist and snug around him.

"Maybe we should think about a condom," she said as the kiss slowly broke.

He'd planned to enjoy foreplay for a while longer but with her mouth working down his throat again and his fuse near ready to blow, he'd go with her "protection now" plan.

Stretching, he lifted the package he'd set earlier on the bedside table. He ripped the wrapping with his teeth and rolled the condom on with Elizabeth on her knees, hovering like a vision above him. His hand was barely away before she took his sheathed length and, maneuvering her hips, gradually eased down and over him.

Sucking in a breath, Daniel grabbed her rump and held

her still. A line of sweat slid from his temple as that internal time bomb ticked and pulsed loud and hard. Eyes squeezed shut, he groaned out a short laugh.

"You want to embarrass me?" *Make me finish too fast.*

"I want to enjoy you. I want you to enjoy me." With his hands on her rear, she began to move. "You have more condoms, don't you?"

Eyes still closed, he smiled. "Oh, yeah."

Her palm slid over his wet forehead as her hips rotated in a slow, sensual circle and, for the first time in living history, Daniel let the bedroom reins slip from his grasp. He'd been sexually physical with the opposite sex in all the best ways. But gazing up into Elizabeth's dreamy face now, something fundamental shifted inside of him. And as the burn of imminent release turned from red to glowing white hot, Daniel was helpless to deny it.

She was unlike anyone he'd ever been with before. Unlike anyone he'd ever met. As his touch trailed up her slender waist and he weighed the perfect curve of each breast, Daniel closed his eyes again and concentrated on the pure heaven about to break.

Thank goodness they had all night.

A noise in the late-night hours woke Daniel from a deep sleep. Blinking into the misty light, he wondered where he was. It came back not in a blinding flash so much as a welcome warm rush. With her perfumed scents drifting over him, he moved carefully onto his side. Elizabeth lay nestled close, curled up, her hands a pillow beneath her cheek.

That warmth stirred and became something deeper and hotter in his chest. He felt the smile on his face as he reached to gently touch her hair, fair and silver threads splayed out in the lifting shadows.

And then he heard the noise again and an unsettling feeling

gripped him. His senses shifted to concentrate. When another scuff sounded, directly below at the front door, he sat bolt upright.

Elizabeth made a sleepy, humming sound and shifted her arms to stretch above her head. Her eyelids fluttered, her gaze found his then her drowsy smile dawned in the dark. Her voice was a sultry drawl that sent his sexual antennae aquiver.

"Hey," she murmured, "I remember you."

He wanted to wrap her up and kiss the inviting words right out of her mouth, but he couldn't dismiss those noises. It was probably a coyote bumping around, but Daniel couldn't stop a snapshot of Bradford Price from creeping into his brain.

*Blackmail... Baby...*

He couldn't shake the unsettled feeling. That noise again.

Heart lurching, he threw off the covers then heard Elizabeth shift, sit up.

"Where are you going?"

"Nowhere. Just outside." On his feet, Daniel found his trousers. He wouldn't bother with the shirt.

"What's outside?"

He held up a warning hand. "Just stay put."

"Daniel, what is it?"

"I don't know. Probably nothing." He came back to dot a kiss on her crown. "I want to make sure."

"Well, you're not going alone."

"For God's sake, Beth, do as I say."

Daniel realized he'd used the shorter, more familiar derivative of her name at the same time she pressed her lips together and threw back the cover, too.

"No."

He wanted to stride off ahead, but, man or woman, this was her property. He couldn't stop her, unless he manacled her to the bed. Hell, that might not even hold her.

On the way out, she grabbed a silk robe off the chaise and, with her lashing the tie, they double-timed it down the stairs. At the bottom, in the dark, she caught his shoulder.

"I'll get a rifle," she whispered.

Daniel recoiled. Not if he could help it. He didn't want a potentially bad situation made worse. And he knew from experience, where guns were involved, things could always get worse.

He shooed her around and close behind. "Just don't go doing anything brave."

Gingerly, he unlocked the door and, as the cool air brushed his skin, he cast a wary glance around the quiet grounds. All seemed routine. The night was tranquil. The low lawn lights shone across strips of grounds. And still, unease rippled up his spine.

Then, way off down the driveway, an engine ignited. A quick flash of headlights as the vehicle hit the main road and then the rumble faded into the distance. Cursing, Daniel thumped the doorjamb. He'd known it wasn't his imagination.

Elizabeth stepped forward and nudged his ribs. "Told you there was nothing to go get all edgy about."

He cocked an eyebrow at her.

"You do realize trespassers just left your property, right?"

Maybe someone who was aware of her sympathies with Abigail's camp and her Yankee architect. Maybe someone who, under the cloak of night, wanted to show Elizabeth she was backing the wrong side.

But Elizabeth only laughed. "They weren't trespassers, silly. Don't you see something missing?"

Daniel had taken a breath, ready to tell her to go back inside so he could call the sheriff, when the truth of what she'd said slapped him upside the head. Turning around, he examined the lawn and sank into himself. Of course, that's what didn't fit. Those blasted flamingos were gone.

*Thank God.* And for more than one reason.

Nonetheless, he wouldn't shake the feeling that something big, bad and unlawful was going down in Royal. Something gritty he wanted nothing to do with. Elizabeth, either.

While he scowled around the parameters, she threaded an arm through his and gave it a tug. "C'mon, cowboy. Let's go inside."

Giving in, he turned, but stopped again when his bare foot met with an object that shouldn't have been there. Frowning, he crouched and collected an envelope. On the front was handwritten scrawl.

*To Elizabeth Milton.*

Grunting, he flipped it over. "Appears someone's desperate to get in touch."

Elizabeth slipped the envelope from his hand, ripping open the seal as they moved into the house. After flicking on some lights, she slid a single sheet out. She read to herself, every so often nodding solemnly.

As the seconds ticked by, Daniel craned to have a look.

"Who's it from?"

She waved the letter as if it were nothing more than a local flyer. "A friend."

"What friend?" he demanded, following as she flicked on more lights and headed down the hall.

"I, er, don't exactly know."

Daniel's hackles went up. If she was in trouble, he wanted to know. And he wanted to know now.

Stopping in the kitchen, he set his fists low on his hips. "I think you'd better tell me."

At the granite island counter, she sized him up as if suddenly, after spending hours of giving herself so completely, she wasn't so sure she could trust him. But then she exhaled. Her slender shoulders in the black silk robe slumped and, setting the letter down, she grabbed the empty coffeepot.

"Someone needs help."

His hands lowered. Now they were getting somewhere.

"Who? What kind of help?"

"A woman and her children." She rinsed the pot and set it back on its perch. "She's from the Midwest. Apparently when her family lost everything in a tornado, her husband lost it, as well. Seems he became physically violent. It was getting worse."

"What's all that got to do with you?"

"That woman and her children escaped and came down here to be near her sister, who's down on her luck at the moment, too. The future looks uncertain, particularly if the husband decides to run her through some rings and take her to court for custody." Scooping out coffee grinds, her voice lowered. "Or decides to take the law into his own hands."

Daniel fought the chill scuttling down his backbone. He made it his business not to think too closely on the subject of broken homes. God knows, there were a lot of them. But this minute, seeing the concern lining Elizabeth's face, it wasn't so easy to pull down his shutter and walk away. Moving around the island to join her, he softened his tone.

"That doesn't explain why you received a letter in the middle of the night."

"It's not common knowledge." She eyed him sternly. "Promise now to not say a word." He swept a finger twice over his heart. "Sometimes when this kind of situation seeps into Royal, the information reaches certain people through the shelter. People who like to give well-deserving individuals a new start, particularly children."

"Certain people being you?"

Setting her jaw, she raised her chin. "I give them some cash, a car, help find them a job if I can." She flicked the percolator on. "I don't advertise."

Daniel lowered his weight onto the nearest kitchen stool

and absorbed the new twist. In this town, secrets went deep and the surprises kept coming. But something didn't add up.

"Your generosity must have limits, particular criteria." He thought she had restraints. "Do you run this by Tremain?"

"He doesn't approve. But he knows it's one of the things that keeps me here." Setting two mugs on the counter, she looked at him. "Don't get me wrong. I love the ranch. But this more than compensates for…"

Her words trailed off.

"For the fact you're caged in five sixths of the year," he finished for her, for the first time truly feeling the ramifications of that sacrifice.

"If I left, I wouldn't lose absolutely everything. I'd still have a trust, but I couldn't help others to the extent I do now."

His heart in his throat, he reached to hold her chin between his thumb and finger then combed the silken hair fallen over one cheek. When her eyes met his he felt his chest swell.

"You're an exceptional woman, you know that?"

Although a thankful smile curved her lips, she denied it. "I'm lucky. I came from a happy home. But there are some who need help to fill in some losses. Mend some wounds. I think of the children," she told him, her voice strong but also filled with compassion. "They need a home. A sense of belonging. It'd be easy, I imagine, to start to run and keep running from a whole pile of things."

The longer he looked at her, the broader his smile grew. Alongside this petite woman, he suddenly felt small.

"You must've been born with a special knack."

"What's that?"

"To help people see that there's more." His lips brushed her forehead and his throat grew tight.

*Help me to see, even a glimpse…*

He cupped her nape and kissed her tenderly, wanting to both convey and absorb what he was feeling. When his lips gradually left hers, he drew in a breath and peered into her vulnerable gaze.

"Do you have any time left this year?"

"Of the two months?"

He nodded.

"Three days."

He rested his forehead on hers. "We can see, and do, a lot in three days."

Then he swept her up and—with her arms around his neck, her head against his shoulder—carried her back upstairs.

# Nine

Elizabeth didn't know how she felt about Daniel Warren. Or rather, she didn't know how she felt about the assortment of maddening emotions he managed to bring out in her.

Early this morning, after the flamingo kidnapping and discovery of the letter asking for help, they'd made love again. Every time he'd stroked and kissed her, the thrills and sense of certainty—or was that *un*certainty—only grew.

With cool wind pushing against her face as Ame thundered down the eastern plain, Elizabeth wondered at the similarities between the way her heart pounded with excitement now and her loss of breath whenever she was with Daniel. His slick dark hair, inviting sexy grin, a body that radiated strength on so many levels…everything about that man reduced her to jelly.

Perhaps it was childish, Elizabeth thought as she cantered in a wide semicircle and headed home, but during those times when she gazed so deeply into his eyes as she lay sated beneath him, the green became an endless ocean she was more than willing to drown in. Whenever his mouth traced the moist line from her cleavage all the way down, she couldn't stop from quivering. Sighing. When his fingertips drifted along her side in the tingling afterglow, she wanted to close her eyes and hold on to that blessed moment forever.

And it frightened her that earlier, when Daniel had gone to work on a design idea, she'd had to bite her lip from begging him to stay.

As Ame galloped again and the wind roared past, Elizabeth tipped back her head and smiled at the warmth of the Texas sun on her face. Daniel made her feel so safe. Interesting and special. He validated her.

He left her wanting more and more.

Ame was hot and lathered by the time she walked him into the stables. Ricquo, a ranch hand, took the reins and offered to brush him down. Elizabeth strolled back to the house, relishing the smells of well-worked horse and sunflowers. But with Daniel offering to take her away for three days, she was ready for a change of scenery. A change of pace.

Biting her lip, she grinned to herself.

Where did he plan to take her?

Her riding boots crunching over gravel, Elizabeth strode up the path thinking Hawaii, Fiji, maybe even Australia. Then she spied an uninvited guest swinging on her back patio seat and spiraling anticipation turned to dread. She didn't want to face that man today, but she should have known he'd show up.

Wanting to get it over with, she straightened her spine and picked up her pace.

"Morning, Chad."

"I see Nita's not around today," he said, pushing out of the swing.

"Gone to see her mother. What can I do for you?"

"I received your correspondence this morning," Chad said in his *I'm disappointed in you* tone. "I needed to tell you in person. I object."

Wiggling out of her gloves, she skirted around him. "I know you do."

They'd had this conversation—confrontation—many times. In fact, every time she instructed Chad to write a check for a family in need. She'd heard all the arguments, and frankly, she was tired of them. But for her parents' sake she'd tell him one more time.

"Through the terms of the will I receive a generous allowance."

She didn't need to involve Chad when lump expenditures came in under a certain amount. But from early on she'd decided not to let that constraint stand in the way of using her allowance when and how she saw fit.

She opened the back door. "My mother would approve of my helping those in need."

"Your father wouldn't. He'd want you to use every cent on assisting the Milton cause—keeping the place running and running well."

Her temper spiked. "My father is *dead.*"

Clenching her gloves in one hand, she sucked down a leveling breath and moved through into the house. She hadn't meant to snap. Neither would she be dictated to. Not one day more.

"Did you write the check?"

Chad answered her question with a question. "Have you made certain this woman's story pans out?"

She had. She always did. But she was tired of playing this game. Of being treated like an infant. Was being in control and keeping her in the realm of "ward" so important to him?

"What is it to you what I do with my allowance? It's not as if I'm gambling or drinking it away."

"You might as well be."

And that's what she hated most about these discussions, she decided, balancing against a wall to heel off her boots. Although he usually kept his feelings low-key and would deny it if asked, Chad was a chauvinist. If she were Ethan Milton's son rather than daughter he wouldn't expect her to have capitulated this long.

She walked away. "I don't wish to discuss it further."

"Then it's settled."

She actually growled. "The only thing that's settled is my impatience with you."

His footfalls followed her into the hall. "Elizabeth, I'll thank you not to address me in that manner."

"I'm not a child."

"You're still vulnerable."

Spinning on him, incredulous, she barked, "Because I'm a single woman?"

His expression changed, softened, and his palms came out as he stepped closer. "I want to look after you."

"I don't *want* to be looked after."

"Listen to me—"

"You listen to *me*. You are my financial advisor for another five years, but there's nothing in that will to say I have to follow your every direction. I've bowed over and again in the past to keep the peace. From this moment on, when I make a decision and give you an instruction, I expect it to be followed without hesitation. Do you understand?"

"You're not thinking straight."

"There is nothing wrong with my mind."

His nostrils flared and voice lowered to a rasp.

"You've slept with him, haven't you?"

Elizabeth didn't stop to think. Her hand drew back then met his face.

Touching the stinging mark rising on his cheek, Chad

nodded as if he knew he deserved it. But, still, he couldn't let it lie.

"Daniel Warren doesn't care a rat's hindquarters for this place. That means he doesn't care about you. Once he earns his money, you won't see him for dust."

"And wouldn't you fall over with fright if I just happened to follow him."

His face paled before a confident smile hooked one side of his mouth. "You wouldn't desecrate your parents' memory like that."

"I'll do whatever I damn well please." Her face hot, tears pickling behind her eyes, she strode off. "Close the door on your way out."

When Nita returned that evening, Elizabeth was sitting cross-legged on the floor in the study, plowing through her old university papers. One hand went behind to help stretch her back as she glanced up and smiled.

"I didn't hear you drive up."

Stepping between the patchwork of textbooks and data sheets, Nita tsked. "That's because you've insulated yourself in here with all this paper. What are you looking for?"

Sighing, Elizabeth sat back on her heels.

*I'm looking for my life.*

"I chose a degree in psychology," she said, collecting her final essay with the excellent grade, "because I wanted to help people."

Bent, about to collect a pile of books, Nita froze. "Has something happened at the shelter?" Nita knew of Elizabeth's work there and how she'd like to do more.

"No." Elizabeth corrected herself. "Not exactly. A woman dropped off a letter here. I asked Chad to organize some funds."

"Oh." Above her glasses, Nita's eyebrows lifted, as if that

explained everything about Elizabeth's low mood. She placed the books on the edge of the ornate 1920s timber desk, which had been Ethan Milton's pride and joy.

"We had our usual tussle," Elizabeth explained, "about whether I was being responsible with my parents' money."

"It's *your* money now."

Still on the floor, Elizabeth blew a stream of air toward the ceiling. Their money. Her money. Wills and caveats and time sliding away. Twenty-five, twenty-six. One day, before she knew it, she'd be Nita's age.

Elizabeth pushed to her feet. "Suddenly I feel so stifled."

"So you've decided to do more study?"

Looking around, she shrugged. "Maybe."

Nita leaned her hips back against the desk, waiting for the younger woman to continue.

Elizabeth wandered to a window and, resting the side of her head against the jamb, looked out on another amazing Texas sunset.

"Daniel came over last night."

"I guessed."

She folded her arms over her nervous stomach. "He makes me feel things I haven't felt before."

"You're falling in love with him?"

*"No."* Elizabeth released the sudden buildup of energy and, thinking more deeply on it, slowly shook her head then smiled. "But I sure like having him around."

"If he gets the job for the club, he'll be in Royal for a while."

"I imagine so." Elizabeth turned to face her friend. "He asked me to go away with him for a couple of days."

Approving, Nita nodded. "When do you leave?"

"I'm not sure. When he left this morning, he had an idea for the design he wanted to work on."

"See what a slice of my cheesecake can do?"

A smile broke across Elizabeth's face. "Imagine if he'd had *two* pieces."

Elizabeth crossed the room and sat behind the desk. A photograph of her grandparents sat on one side in a solid silver frame. Another of her mother and father on their wedding day sat on the other. Both shots had been taken out front of this house.

Elizabeth collected the wedding day shot and felt her throat swell with emotion. Whenever the *miss you* feeling got too much, she liked to look through old photographs, although she was never sure if it made her feel better or worse.

"Daniel doesn't like his parents," she murmured, running a fingertip down the train of her mother's wedding gown. "He dislikes his memories of the South even more."

"The past is important. We need to understand where we come from," Nita said in her wise rather than wisecrack voice. "But we need to remember that the future is ours to create."

"Is it?" Setting down the photo, Elizabeth imagined a similar shot of her with a proud Texan husband. "Or is it mapped out for us?" Plotted with a few twists and turns before an inevitable conclusion?

"I've decided to see more of my mother," Nita said. "Stay more regularly."

Elizabeth's gaze snapped up. "Not to give Daniel and me more space here?"

"I'd already decided." Her lips twitched. "Although he is a nice boy."

"He's a busy set-in-his-ways-millionaire-passing-through boy." Elizabeth slumped. "And I'm a restless heiress with too much time on her hands."

"You're a man and a woman."

"It feels wrong to want something I know I can never have. And yet when we're together, it feels so right."

"Go away with Daniel. Enjoy your time." Nita sauntered toward the door. "The ranch will be here when you get back."

Folding her forearms on the desk, Elizabeth bent forward to study the papers strewn across the floor. Then she remembered Chad's unacceptable behavior and all the women from the shelter she'd helped in the past. Finally she remembered Daniel, his wicked smile, scorching embraces. His offer of escape.

Her stomach sinking, Elizabeth laid her head on her folded arms.

*What if she never wanted to come back?*

# Ten

Elizabeth was curious when she didn't hear from Daniel the rest of the day, but when flowers appeared on her doorstep the next morning, her heart leaped. She was sure he'd dropped off the gorgeous handpicked bunch of wild blooms. But when she ripped open the small card, she learned she was mistaken.

It read simply:

*Thank you for making such a difference.*

She slowly lowered the card. Not from Daniel. Still the warmth unfurling around her heart at the sentiment swam up to form a big smile. Seemed the flowers were from the sister of the woman she'd helped. She must have received the check Elizabeth had collected from Chad's office and dropped at the shelter late yesterday. Good. Elizabeth hoped she would be kept up-to-date on that family's progress from time to time, on how the days, months and even years ahead unfolded.

Midmorning, Elizabeth went for a long ride, checking cattle and fences until almost noon. She investigated study options until one o'clock, but the whole time she couldn't help watching the phone. When Daniel still hadn't called by two, she put pride aside and dressed to go into town.

Thirty minutes later, her pewter Shelby Cobra curved into the town's main street. She parked directly in front of the Royal Hotel but then, for a good ten minutes, she simply sat, wringing the sports steering wheel, gnawing her lower lip. She didn't want to look desperate and knock on her architect's door a second time. But she couldn't sit here all day, either. And she couldn't stop wondering…

Why hadn't he called? Had something happened with Abigail and his idea for a new design? Was he still in town, or had Daniel left without telling her?

Her heart knocking at her ribs, Elizabeth studied her cell, lying in her purse on the seat alongside of her. She could call Abigail, ask a few subtle questions. Oh, but that seemed beyond lame, too. She and Daniel had spent an amazing day together. He'd said he'd take her away. She couldn't believe that invitation had been nothing more than pillow talk.

Or was she as vulnerable—naive—as Chad would have her believe?

Outside, Brad Price appeared, strolling down Main with new Texas Cattleman Zeke Travers, who, word had it, was also a consultant for Brad's security firm. On the other side of the street, Addison Harper was holding court with poor Rosaline Jamestown, who glanced over and recognized the car. Sliding down in the driver's seat, a chill raced over Elizabeth's skin. Eyes and ears were everywhere. She didn't care if she was seen with Daniel. To hell with anyone who didn't like that the Cattleman's Club was being redefined and updated after a hundred years. But she did not want to be seen chasing after a man. She'd rather never hear from Daniel again. She had her pride, after all.

Making a quick decision, she rammed into Reverse and

stepped on the gas, ready to drive away. The jolt from her back bumper hurled her forward against her belt at the same instant the crunch of metal on metal echoed through the car and her heart jumped to the top of her throat. Elizabeth threw a wild glance behind her and withered. Of all the people to run into, and this way.

Her face burning, she set her forehead on the steering wheel. She couldn't bring herself to get out and explain.

A rap on the window forced her to edge her gaze higher over the wheel. Daniel Warren was grinning in at her, signaling for her to lower the window.

"Fancy bumping into you here," he said, looking amused as he leaned folded forearms on the ledge when the window was down.

She fought the urge to pat her warm cheeks. "I apologize. I...I didn't see your vehicle."

His Adam's apple bobbed as he laughed. "You didn't look." His gaze searched hers before dropping to devour her lips. "Anything special bring you into town?"

"Special?" While her heartbeat skipped on, she pretended to think. "Just a few errands."

"At the hotel?"

His devilish, knowing grin had her dissolving. There was no use pretending. Angling her head, she sat back.

"Truth is I was curious."

"About my design?"

She nodded. *And other things.*

He swung open her door, but she hesitated. "Are you sure you have time?"

"I always have time for you."

Before heading off, Daniel checked the negligible damage to their cars then, taking her arm, he escorted her around folk meandering down the footpath—some clearly interested in the pair—and into the hotel foyer. As they entered the building's cool interior, Elizabeth's stomach knotted and she slid a look around. Just the day before yesterday, after she and Daniel had made love, she'd bumped into Chad here. But surely lightning didn't strike twice in one place.

When they were in the privacy of an elevator, Daniel wasted no time in rotating her to face him. His palms gliding down the sensitive indentation of her back, he gathered her near and kissed her thoroughly while she melted into a grateful, pliant puddle. The time spent waiting, wondering if she might have dreamed those hours spent together, had been worth every minute.

The world was spinning when the elevator doors opened. Still, Daniel took his sweet time breaking the kiss. When his mouth finally left hers, his lips remained teasingly close. Dizzy, Elizabeth clung to his shirt, imagining the hard flesh steaming beneath as his hooded, hungry gaze searched hers.

"You're addictive."

Floating, she leaned in. "Feeling's mutual."

"We're still on for an escape from Royal then?"

She almost buckled with relief. He hadn't forgotten.

"Anytime you're ready."

Hot, strong fingers laced through hers as they stepped into the corridor and headed toward his door.

"I want to get the basics of the new design sorted first. I'll send scans to Rand so he can work on the dimensions and scaled drawings."

"Don't you want to do that yourself?"

"When I've sketched everything out, I intend to spend time with you."

"You might be missing New York by then."

"Is that a hint? Do you want to spend our days visiting the Statue of Liberty and Central Park?"

"If you really want to know, I have a craving for something far more private. Maybe something tropical."

Swiping the keycard, he winked. "Leave it to me."

Inside the suite, they crossed to a long central table. Sketches were scattered everywhere so that only snatches of wood poked through. When something crunched beneath her foot, Elizabeth looked down. Paper lay all over the floor, too.

After clearing a square, he positioned a sheet in the center of the table and stood back, hands low on his hips.

"Tell me if you think it'll fly."

Stepping up, she inspected the drawings. There were scales and numbers and different angles. Confusing for a layperson, but the overall concept was clear and, to her mind, nothing short of perfect!

At her side, he slipped slim reading glasses on then ran two fingertips over the main drawing.

"Exterior material will be stone but also with a strong emphasis on glass, which will encase a tall tunnel ceiling spanning the entire length of the curving building."

"Lots of glass…to let the light in?"

"Natural light," he agreed, his attention on the drawing. "Light coming from the new membership and century."

Smiling at the excitement sparkling in his eyes, she nodded then looked down again.

"And this shape?"

"I couldn't get away from the symbol that most typifies this state as well as the club. Plastering massive steer horns on a giant cowhide door, however, was one of my less inspired ideas."

Elizabeth only pressed her lips together. Everyone made mistakes.

"But here the symbol of the club," he went on, "steer horns, are embodied within the structure of the building itself. The character of the Cattleman's Club is everywhere without being in anyone's face."

The building had no sharp angles or corners but rather curved around, in and out again, mimicking a set of horns. She pointed out the semicircular spaces.

"What'll go in here?"

"I'm not sure yet. But I have an idea for the separate sections of the club with regard to color." He pointed to the drawing. "That wing or horn will be devoted to equitable gatherings, such as sport, which should inspire a sense of fair play—or justice, if you will. It will be decorated with black opals in mind."

"Black leather and granite trims?" she asked.

"Shimmering surfaces. The center third will be dining, meeting rooms and the library. The leadership area's decor will reflect the legend's red diamond."

"Like red granite, redwood trimming and crimson carpet."

"Uh-huh. The other wing…" He inhaled, slipped off his glasses and straightened. "Well, I'm still working out what to put in there but the theme will be emeralds. Green for growth."

"And for peace."

He smiled. "Right."

She studied the design a final time then, satisfied, drew back. "If you're going to get this done on time, I'd best let you be."

His arm scooped around her waist and unapologetically tugged her in, deliciously close to his heady, innate heat.

"You're not going anywhere," he growled.

"I'm not?"

"Not today." His head angled until his lips brushed hers, back and forth, up and blissfully down. Lower, she felt the physical result of his desire press against her belly and a wonderful floating feeling fell over her. Her next words came out a sigh.

"I didn't bring anything with me."

"What do you need?" His head lowered and he kissed her neck as if he were tasting fruits sent from heaven. "This." He changed to the other side. "Or this?"

Gripping his broad shoulders, she liquefied more.

"You could wear a lady out," she murmured.

A second before his mouth claimed hers, he admitted, "Or die trying."

After two weeks of drawing and consulting with Abigail, Daniel was happy with his new design. He sent everything up to Rand to mark up the final drawings and to create a presentation, and then he told Elizabeth to get her beach gear and passport together. His private jet was fueled and waiting to fly them away.

During the flight out, he kept quiet about their destination. While she sat back in the leather seat, looking exquisite in a pretty yellow sundress and matching sandals, he wondered if she'd approve of his choice of location. Then again, she had asked for private.

Throughout the jet's descent and when they touched down on an isolated tarmac, Elizabeth seemed breathless with excitement. Clear blue skies, a jungle of palms, riots of colorful island blooms. She held her cheeks.

"This is brilliant!"

"This Caribbean island's very small, very private." He grazed his lips against her temple. "Very romantic." As they moved toward the door, he confessed, "I thought about the Pacific Islands, but I didn't want to waste too much time in the air."

When she smiled at him, understanding, he felt compelled to add, *There's always next year.* But he didn't want to jump the gun. No doubt they'd enjoy their time here together, but he wouldn't go making any plans in advance. He would still need to stay in Royal on and off if he got the job. If that were the case he'd be more than happy to continue to see Elizabeth. But if his design wasn't successful, fact was, soon he'd be back in New York. And Elizabeth would be stuck down South.

Not anyone's fault. Nothing either of them could change. That circumstance merely reinforced the obvious. He wasn't into long-distance affairs. He avoided them as much as ground glass in his oats. They should enjoy the time they had now.

A woman wearing a bright multicolored shirt and flowers in her dark hair greeted them. After collecting luggage, they were driven in a four-wheel drive to their lodgings—a thatched roof bungalow perched on the edge of an idyllic stretch of long white beach. Elizabeth audibly sighed as she moved through the front door, across the main room decorated with rattan furniture, then out onto a massive balcony, which overlooked sparkling shallow waters that journeyed out toward an endless turquoise sea.

"What's this place called?"

"It's a private island owned by a friend," he said, his hand coming to rest on the small of her back as he joined her. "Sinbad Isle."

She swung to him, her eyes bright. "Does it have a history of pirates? Of treasure?"

He laughed. "I vote we explore and find out." Maybe they could start their own legend.

"Have you been here before?"

"I've had the offer for some time but I've never taken my friend up on it."

"Are we the only ones here?"

"Aside from the caretakers, who have their own quarters on the other side of the island, we're completely alone."

With a wicked grin, she kicked off her sandals. "There's something I want to try."

"What's that?"

"Take off your clothes and I'll show you."

Daniel wanted to pinch himself as Elizabeth proceeded to wriggle out of her sundress. When she got down to her fiery orange mini bikini, he snapped back and wound, double time, out of his shirt. Then she reached around her nape, pulled the tie and those two orange triangles of fabric fell to her hand-span waist. When his brain began to swim, Daniel remembered to breathe.

"You'd like to try out the bed?"

"No, silly." She shimmied out of her bottoms, too. "I want to try out the water."

Elizabeth left Daniel standing on the balcony with his jaw dropped and boxers ready to do the same.

She flew down the half-dozen wooden stairs and out along the warm, soft sand with not a stitch on. With the sun high and warm, she let out a laugh as her feet smacked the cool water. She'd waded out farther and was about to dive into the shallows when an arm lassoed her waist and brought them both down.

Water closed in over her head before hands, settled on her waist, jettisoned her up into the air and she heard Daniel's laughter join her own. When she landed, she tried to escape again, but he caught her from behind and, her legs sending out fans of water, swung her around.

"You, Miss Milton, are a wild child. Are you known for this kind of behavior back home?"

"It might surprise you," she told him over her bare shoulder, "but this is my first time running naked down a tropical island beach."

"I'm glad I was here to see it."

With them both out of breath, he rotated her around in the circle of his arms. His steamy palms slid down her back as he pressed her against his hard, beating chest.

"I guess now's the time to admit," he said, "that for some strange reason I'm not feeling much like swimming."

"Who said anything about swimming?"

Her fingers slid down and, one by one, wrapped around his throbbing length while Daniel's eyes widened.

With the incoming tide coursing around them, he lifted her inch by inch until her legs coiled around his hips and locked behind his back. Her wet hair hanging over his face, she nipped his bottom lip then, holding his head, captured his mouth with hers. She felt his heart hammering like an overworked piston by the time she let him go. His gaze on her lips, he hummed in his throat.

"You don't mind if we shock a few seagulls then?"

Legs still coiled around his back, she'd moved on to nibbling his earlobe.

"You're not going all shy on me, I hope." When he eased her slightly down, the tip of his erection nudged inside of her and she sucked down a startled breath. Then, raveling her arms around his neck, she expelled a long, loving sigh. "I guess not."

With him holding her in place, she moved as he moved—around him, with him—and let the syrupy warmth spread through her as his mouth grazed her forehead, her cheeks, her ever-welcoming mouth. With him filling more of her, she embraced the thrust of his tongue and the tease as his damp chest hair tickled her breasts. Soon she was left catching her breath and softly repeating his name.

When the beginnings of a contraction quivered low in her belly, she buried her face in the hot, corded sweep of his neck. Her muscles clamped around him and her mind went deliciously blank as she started to tremble and her every fiber pulsed. As her lit fuse finally ran out, a storm of sparks flew and the fire at the heart of her broke free.

Her legs squeezed him closer, urged him deeper as her

orgasm gripped again and again. But in the recesses of her mind, she was vaguely aware of Daniel cursing softly. And then, in her daze, she understood.

He wasn't wearing protection.

As she clung to him still, he murmured against her jaw.

"You took me by surprise. Then again, you always do."

She curled a fingertip around his sandpaper jaw and whispered near his lips, "Take me inside."

He angled her around until she lay cradled in his arms and he walked them out of the water. When they reached the bungalow, he set her down, found a condom then led her to a spacious double shower surrounded by luminous ferns and slats of bamboo. Beneath the warm spray they soaped each other up, washed each other down, and when the sensations got too much, he made love to her—protected this time—his palm on the glass beside her head, while the water hissed and streamed around them.

Later, with big, fluffy towels, they patted each other dry. While Elizabeth found her hairbrush, hungry, Daniel checked out the well-stocked fridge. He came back to the bedroom with a platter overflowing with fruit, cheese and bread. After setting the banquet down on the bed, which was strewn with sweet-smelling flowers, he made a second trip, returning with a chilled bottle of champagne.

He took a flourishing bow. "Luncheon is served."

Elizabeth crawled to the middle of the bed, popped a plump purple grape into his mouth and another into her own. Sweet juice bursting in her mouth, she rolled down onto the bed and wriggled into the covers.

"I've died and gone to heaven."

"When was your last break from Royal?"

"Beginning of the year. A lovely, long skiing vacation in Canada and a shorter trip to the South of France. I visited some friends in L.A., too." She rocked up to slice off some Camembert. "Time went way too quickly."

"Do your friends come down to visit?"

"Sure. But college days were different. It was like we were part of a big family. My L.A. friend, Kayla, is like a sister to me." She accepted a glass of champagne. "When I was younger, I used to bug Mom nonstop for a sister of my own." Grinning, she raised her glass. "Even a brother."

"Yeah. Me, too."

"Really?"

"I mean I wish I still had a brother." His eyebrows pulled together. "My parents had a second child after I was born. Jonas died when he was eight."

The news hit her in the chest and, for a long moment, Elizabeth could only gape. She'd had no idea.

"I thought you were an only child," she said, "like me."

"Not initially."

She put her next grape down. "Would you like to tell me about him?"

Daniel gazed into his glass and she knew he was thinking back, deciding whether or not to open up.

"Well, he was a gentle soul," he said finally. "Always trying to stick up for one or the other of our parents." His smile came slowly. "And he could make me laugh. He used to put on shows, dancing and singing and clowning around. He liked to paint, too." He sent her a quick look. "Mom wanted to give him lessons. Dad said it would make him more of a sissy than he already was. Our father would have preferred we both follow in his esteemed footsteps."

Forcing himself to remember, he joined her to sit on the edge of the bed.

"We were due to visit Carolina," he went on, "when I came down with tonsillitis, so Jonas went on his own. The chauffeur picked him up, the jet flew him down, another limo drove him to the mansion and…" His jaw tensed and his throat burned. "I never saw him again."

She held his hand. "What happened?"

"The old man wanted to take him hunting. Jonas would do anything to make his father happy, except that. Still he dragged him along. There was an accident. If I didn't hate that SOB before—"

When she put her arms around him, Daniel took a moment then said, "I've never told another living soul that story."

He wasn't sure how he felt about sharing it even now. He kept a photo of himself and Jonas in his bottom drawer at work. But he purposely hadn't looked at it in years. Moping over photos wouldn't change anything. He'd rather just try to blot it from his memory. Try to cover and bury the wound.

"Anyway, that's all in the past."

"The past makes us who we are. The future's ours to create," she said with a wisdom that made him look twice.

But, "I'm *living* my future," he reminded her, then downed a mouthful of bubbles. "I have everything I need."

"If you say so," she muttered.

He eyed her almost pitying expression and gave in to a short laugh.

"What's so wrong about letting go of the past?" he asked. "Better than hanging blindly on to it."

Living with regret and anger and wanting to slam someone in the jaw.

"Daniel, my situation and yours are completely different."

He huffed under his breath. "Damn right they are."

When she drew away, hurt, he cursed himself a thousand ways and reached for her hand. He normally didn't let the past, those suffocating emotions, get to him for precisely this reason. Right or wrong, it got the better of him. He hadn't meant to diminish the pain in her past.

"I'm sorry." His thumb rubbed the underside of her wrist. "I can't imagine how it feels to lose your parents."

She tried to hide the upset from her face and, gracious as ever, said, "I can't imagine what it would be like to lose a sibling."

*It was the worst pain I've ever lived through. Something I never intend to experience again. For anyone. For any reason.*

Suddenly that food he'd been salivating for no longer seemed appetizing. Instead he took her glass, set both aside then brought her to lie beside him while he snuggled her in.

He loved every minute of being with Elizabeth. He was happy he'd brought her here, and yet there was a part of this situation he *didn't* like. He was afraid she might want to change him, and that wouldn't happen. He was scared she'd end up wanting more. Maybe "forever." He wasn't in a position to do that. Risk himself that way.

Even if a part of him wished he could.

# Eleven

They lay together with the quiet of the island wrapping around them and Elizabeth pondering a much younger Daniel standing at the foot of his little brother's grave. He blamed his father for Jonas's death and had never forgiven him. She felt ill imagining the anguish that had made a horrible rift within the family that much more difficult to repair.

As he stroked her hair and every so often dropped a kiss on her crown, she felt torn. She wanted to help him, as she tried to help the families who came to her in need. But for Daniel, her money wouldn't make a difference. He had enough of his own. More than he could spend in three lifetimes. Daniel's problem was far worse.

He might pretend that he had his past sorted, but he was filled with resentment, so much so that it didn't take much for the bitterness and mistrust to come pouring out. Daniel Warren had grown to be a man who needed to keep a firm grip on his own fate, and that meant avoiding what had survived of his family.

Had he ruled out having a family of his own?

Later, they nibbled at the platter's fare then dressed, donned sneakers and headed off inland to explore. Meandering over sandy ground, marveling at the colorful birdlife peering curiously down at them, she and Daniel stopped when they heard a distant w*hooshing* sound. They resumed walking and a few minutes later a picturesque waterfall and crystal-clear pond came into view. Giant water lilies floated in tranquil patterns, and ancient-looking boulders dotted the pond's boundaries. Elizabeth couldn't wait to feel the soft, pure water against her skin.

"It looks like something out of a movie." She inhaled and sighed. "It smells so fresh."

As they trekked nearer, Daniel angled to get a better view and then pointed. "I think there's a cave behind the waterfall."

"A pirate-type cave?" Her pulse spiking, Elizabeth crept nearer. "Maybe there's a treasure."

He set down their backpack of provisions and grabbed her hand. "Let's find out."

With a choir of birdcalls radiating throughout the canopies of palm fronds and tropical perfume filling their lungs, they skirted around the perimeter of the pond and its boulders. The rush of water grew closer until finally they stood before a swift vertical stream. Spray clung to their hair and dotted their clothes as they tried to see past the fall to the cave in the cliff behind. Daniel had to raise his voice to be heard over the roar.

"You game?"

Navigating the slimy ledge, she pushed past him. "Darn right I am."

She heard Daniel calling for her to wait, and as the rock beneath her rubber soles grew more treacherous, she did, setting a palm against the cold cliff wall to steady herself. Over the rush, he shouted near her ear.

"Take it easy. We have all day."

Actually, she had *two* days here with Daniel. Before they flew back to Royal, she wanted to enjoy every adventurous minute to the hilt.

When the rock curved in, forming a shelter in the cliff from the spray and some of the noise, she moved to wipe down her drenched face. When her footing slipped and heart catapulted to her throat, Daniel lunged. His grip on her arm might leave a bruise but it had kept her from falling into the drink unprepared.

"Why don't I go first," he called, looking mock stern as he overtook her. "Hold on to my belt."

Elizabeth grinned. She liked that he wanted to protect her but she couldn't let the opportunity slide. "So now *you* think I need looking after?" she asked, remembering their earlier conversation that had revolved around Chad Tremain.

He looked back over his shoulder. A shadow crossed his face before he returned her smug smile. "Special circumstances."

They edged deeper inside the rock-walled shelter until the temperature dropped to chilly and the crash of water falling receded to a far-off echoing rush. Scooping back wet hair clinging to her cheeks, she squinted around. Stray prisms of light threw relief on areas but it was too dark to see if any pirate chests lay half buried nearby.

Daniel's deep voice reverberated off the tunnel walls.

"Can't see any Spanish gold glittering at our feet."

"Maybe if we go farther in."

She crept off deeper toward the slanting shadows and the unknown.

After a few minutes, he said, "We should have brought a flashlight."

"You're not getting nervous, are you?"

"Me? I happen to think bats are cute."

Blinking in the dark, she pulled up. "Bats?"

"Must be some interesting species of cave spiders in here, too."

A vision of things big, black and hairy falling on her head filled Elizabeth's brain and a run of shivers scuttled up her spine. But then she swallowed the lump of fear, threw back her wet shoulders and inched farther in. Soon the smell of damp was beaten only by the constant trickling drip down limestone.

Daniel's hand tightened around hers. "Had enough yet?"

At the same time he spoke, a distant squeak filtered down through the dark. Or maybe she imagined it. Either way, the vision of black wings beating toward them finally got the better of her.

"Well, if you really want to go…"

In the shadows, she heard him chuckle.

When they reached the ledge again, this side of the waterfall but far enough away not to have to shout, Elizabeth sat down, pumped and happy.

"Wasn't that fun?"

He lowered down beside her. "If I'm not mistaken, Miss Milton, you're a bit of an adrenaline junkie."

"Only when it's available."

"You're not into white-water rafting, by any chance? Climbing Eiger's north face?"

"Not yet."

"What about bull riding?"

"Only if Daddy wasn't watching."

"He liked to keep you good and safe."

Truth was that her father liked to keep her under lock and key. As rich as they were, if it weren't for her mother she'd never have got the chance to board overseas, see and learn what she had. But then Elizabeth thought of Daniel's father, putting Jonas in danger, and felt ashamed. His father had been reckless with his children's safety and the Warren family had paid the ultimate price.

*I guess there's a balance,* she conceded, trying to see past the fall of water. It was up to each individual to find it.

"What would you think if I said I had thought about ignoring the will?" she admitted. "About simply walking away."

Daniel looked at her as if she'd said she wanted to sell Manhattan to the Queen of Mars.

"I'd say Tremain would have a fit."

She threw a rock at the water. "I don't care what Chad thinks."

"He cares about you. And more than a financial advisor should." She shot him a glance. "Guys know these things."

She looked away. She couldn't help if fortysomething Chad would like something more from their relationship. She'd never given him any reason to believe she felt the same way. As far as she was concerned, the only reason they spoke on a regular basis was because of the ranch. That was what she needed to do to keep her inheritance.

"I never would, of course," she told him, carrying on her thread. "Leave the ranch, I mean. I could never simply walk away."

"Although you might not believe me, I understand."

She blinked across. "You do?"

"I'll never leave New York."

While water continued to spray their already damp clothes and course down their faces, he looked at her steadily. But he didn't manage to stare her down. They both knew where the other stood. They were both adults and they hadn't come here to analyze each other. They were here to have a good time.

She pushed to her feet and, carefully, they edged back

out into the dappled sunshine. After spreading out a blanket near the pond, they picnicked on chicken and potato salad, listening to the different hoots and clicks while discussing plans for the morrow.

"It's hard to believe we were in Royal this morning," she said, looking around the tropical setting for the hundredth time.

"You missing it?"

She sent a sly look. "No."

"Have you got any more stories I should hear?" He sat up and scooped together some stones and leaves. "Anything scandalous?" he asked, thinking of Bradford Price.

"About the Cattleman's Club?" He nodded, making a small base, or floor, with the stones. "The Club is all about public service. Honor and duty. There was talk that they broke up a black-market baby organization."

His hand hesitated, starting on a stone wall.

*Black-market babies.*

"Is that a fact?"

"It's said they helped stop a bloody overthrow of a European principality," she went on. "And there's the stories surrounding the feud between the Windcrofts and the Devlins, two of Royal's most prominent families. But I'm particularly fond of the legend surrounding Jessamine Golden."

"Was she an heiress?"

"An outlaw who is reputed to be an ancestor of our own Abigail Langley. She stole a pile of gold. It must have been around 1900. She was in love with the sheriff but when he rode off to bring her in, he disappeared. The mayor went after him. Later, he and all his men were found dead. A discovery was made a few years ago. Saddlebags, a purse, a set of six-shooters and a map, which was supposed to have belonged to Jessamine."

"Was *supposed* to have belonged to her?"

"It was authenticated by our Historical Society Museum's historian and was reported to be 'an exceptional and significant find.'"

"And the missing gold?"

"A few years back, the Cattleman's Club was involved in a mystery, and murder, surrounding that map, which was meant to lead to her gold. But, far as I know, none was ever found."

Daniel put one too many stones on his wall and it all fell down. He dusted his hands.

"Sounds like you ought to set up your own treasure hunt around Royal."

She gave a wicked grin as she leaned over for a kiss. "Maybe I'll do that."

That evening, they dined on fresh crawfish and all manner of exotic fruits. Daniel found a sound system and, after cleaning the table, they danced beneath an ocean of glittering stars. When his mouth found hers and he kissed her in the moonlight, Elizabeth was taken aback to feel the threat of tears sting behind her eyes. When she was young, time seemed inconsequential. Now it either dragged or flew by. Right now it was racing.

They made love in a lazy way that left Elizabeth only longing for more. When she opened her eyes early the next morning, she sat up in surprise. The last thing she remembered was Daniel leaving the bedroom around midnight to get two glasses of water. The day's adventure—and romance—must have taken more energy than she'd thought.

After a leisurely breakfast of eggs, fruit and pastries, they played volleyball across a net provided on the beach, waded knee deep in the tide, laughing whenever a friendly stingray fluttered past their legs, then went for a long swim before a relaxed lunch and afternoon nap, although they didn't get much sleep.

Late afternoon, they emerged again. The island was cooler and particularly quiet.

"It's like another world," she said, as they sat with tall, cool drinks on the balcony, gazing over the shimmering blue waters that would hopefully never know the word *civilization.*

"You wouldn't rather be in Rome or London or Singapore? The shopping's excellent there, so I've heard." He leaned close and stole a lingering kiss from the corner of her lips. "Or maybe bungee jumping off an African precipice."

"You're just old and staid," she joked back.

"And you're beautiful."

The teasing smile in his eyes faded and Elizabeth swore it had been replaced by his heart.

But then awareness seeped back into his expression. He drew slowly away and, looking around, nodded toward the left. "I vote this afternoon we explore that way."

Elizabeth was still gathering herself, quelling the butterflies released in the pit of her stomach.

"I second the motion," she said, telling herself to hold it together. Yes, they were having an extraordinary time here alone, with New York and Royal left far behind. But no matter what they were feeling, tomorrow meant a return to reality. She'd best not forget that.

Slipping on hats, they walked along the edge of the water, around the horseshoe bay, over a patchwork of rock, which had been flattened and smoothed by millennia of gentle waves. The headland terrain petered out to sheltered mud lands where the occasional crab scuttled past.

In the near distance, Elizabeth spotted movement...precise, elegant. It was a bird, about five feet tall. Its plumage was a magnificent orange-pink. She covered her mouth to contain the gasp turned laugh.

"Look." She shook her hand at the form picking its way over the flats. "A real-life flamingo."

Daniel shaded his eyes. "Well, I'll be. A little different from the plastic jobs they dropped on your lawn."

She inched forward. "I wonder if there's more."

Careful not to alarm the bird, they edged closer. But it seemed the flamingo wasn't up for an audience. On stick legs, it walked slowly away.

Daniel caught her elbow. "We should probably leave him be."

Elizabeth considered it but then shook her head. The smells of the ocean, the sea breeze tugging through her hair, a gorgeous man who'd opened this world to her at her side... she didn't want to waste any opportunity.

"Let's see where he goes."

With a grin, Daniel surrendered and they followed the bird, the soles of their shoes sticking and smacking at the ground. When they rounded that corner, Elizabeth's heart fell.

"He's gone."

Daniel's arm came around her and rubbed her shoulder. "Guess we were lucky to have spotted him at all."

Like she'd been lucky to happen upon Daniel, a splash of color in her life when she hadn't let herself acknowledge she'd needed it.

Elizabeth squeezed shut her eyes. After their time here, she didn't know how she'd keep her decorum when the time came to say goodbye. Her two months would be renewed come January, but would Daniel want to spend any of that time with her? He was a busy man with his own busy life. He probably had an army of women with exactly the same wish as hers.

His hold on her arm tightened. His voice was an urgent whisper at her ear.

"Quick, *look*."

She opened her eyes at the same time he angled her a little to her right. A flash of orange-pink appeared amid the foliage, and another flash. Her heart beating fast again, she moved closer, Daniel at her side. She held her hands over her sigh at the sight greeting them.

"It's a whole flock," he said.

"Young ones, too." She sniffed at the emotion tickling behind her nose. "It's the most beautiful thing I've ever seen."

Suddenly she felt alive. Raised up. Different from galloping down a plain. Better than dining at the best Parisian cafés. And she had to wonder…

The sight was an amazing one, but did it feel so surreal, so special, because Daniel was here beside her?

Was she the only one falling in love?

# Twelve

The jet returned to the island to collect him and Elizabeth midmorning the next day. Daniel could have stayed another week. *Two*. Looking at Elizabeth's sun-kissed stoic face now as she boarded the aircraft, he knew she felt the same way.

He'd like to think there'd be a next time. But, given her present circumstance with regard to two months' vacation only per year, he hadn't wanted to dangle another invitation. There were still several more weeks until the new year. A lot could happen in that time. If he were perfectly honest, he liked Elizabeth way too much to risk hurting her. No matter how good she made him feel—and she made him feel *amazing*— they had no future. He didn't want long-term, a wife. Didn't want children of his own. He would not put himself in a situation where he could risk losing a family again. If that made him pessimistic, so be it.

Even if he was the marrying kind, he couldn't see himself living out his days cowpoke-ing around down South. The wild side of Elizabeth might feel trapped by her parents' will, but she'd made clear she intended to stick it out and stand by her decision to hold on to her ranch. His hat went off to her. But his life—business and personal—revolved around New York City.

While Elizabeth was relatively young, soon enough she'd be thinking about finding a husband. He wasn't that man. No use pretending he was. Hell, it might even be better for his design to get the thumbs-down from the Cattleman's Club pronto and speed up the inevitable. He could fly out and be back up North for good in a matter of days.

The flight from the island back to Texas was a quiet one. Elizabeth seemed as deeply entrenched in reflection as he was. When they touched down in Royal, the mood was vastly different from when they'd left.

"I'll drop you off at the ranch," he said in a manufactured, breezy tone as Elizabeth slid into the back passenger seat of the chauffeur-driven Benz he'd organized to meet them. "I need to catch up on things back at the hotel."

She looked up at him with hope-filled eyes. "Would you like to come over for dinner tonight?"

Yes, he did. A little too much. Which meant he needed to back right off and take some time out for them both to catch their breath and get reacclimatized to reality.

"Can I take a rain check?" he asked, sliding into the leather- and wood-trimmed cabin beside her. "I don't know how long I'll be on conference with Rand. I might even get him to fly down again. Or I might fly up to see what he's done."

As he buckled up, she blinked over a wry smile. "Fly back to New York? *Now?*"

"That's where my office is," he said, using his matter-of-fact tone.

"I know. It's just..." She swallowed the rest and peered out her window. "Never mind."

The drive to Milton Ranch was another silent affair. He tried to engage Elizabeth in conversation but it seemed that etiquette had taken the day off. The mood inside the car mimicked the landscape outside, Daniel thought, watching stunted trees on near-naked plains whiz by. Compared to the scenery they'd lapped up these past days on the island, Royal was a desert.

When the car pulled up front of the ranch, the chauffeur opened the passenger back door but Daniel insisted on carrying Elizabeth's luggage and asked the chauffeur to drive around the side to wait.

"You can set them down there," she said, when they reached the front door. A pair of glittering green eyes tipped up to meet his. "Thank you, Daniel, for taking me away. I really did have a wonderful time."

"Wish it could've been longer."

"Maybe we can do it again sometime," she said, taking the lead.

Daniel searched for an answer that would neither insult nor commit. He nodded, smiled and rasped out, "Sure."

A voice filtered down the hall. "Beth? Is that you?"

At the sound of Nita's voice, Daniel snapped back from wanting to kiss Elizabeth deeply one last time at the same moment the Milton Ranch housekeeper appeared at the doorway, with her glasses slipping down her nose and a hearty smile ready to greet them. She set a kiss on Elizabeth's cheek and bounced on tiptoe to make certain he didn't miss out. Relishing the warm feeling in his chest, Daniel touched his face. If he had a grandmother he kept in touch with, he'd have liked her to be like Nita. What you saw was what you got, and it was all good.

"Just in time for some of my Texas Sheet Cake." Nita

looped an arm through his and drew him inside. "You like crushed pecans and chocolate?"

Daniel hunted for an excuse. He wanted to put some distance between himself, Elizabeth and any expectations she might have developed. But he failed to come up with one, especially when Elizabeth was looking so pleased he'd decided to "come in." So, surrendering, he was drawn to the scrumptious-smelling kitchen, his favorite room in the house.

While he and Elizabeth got comfortable around the table, Nita expertly cut then slipped cake onto separate plates.

"Fresh out of the oven." Setting the plates down in front of the pair, she asked, "How was the break?"

"We saw *flamingos,*" Elizabeth announced, picking off a pecan and slipping it into her mouth. "Real ones. And we explored a pirate's cave for treasure."

Nita chuckled. "You sound like a kid at Christmas." She flicked on the coffeepot. "How about you, Daniel? Have you come back revitalized?"

"It was a great escape," he admitted, pleased to see Elizabeth animated again.

Nita's cake was a bonus. He did have to make contact with Rand, but he was certain his assistant would have everything under control. It was nice to be able to push back responsibility a little longer. Pretend he could do this—be with Elizabeth—every week if he wanted.

Remembering something, Nita clapped her hands. "You got some interesting mail this morning, Beth. A lady dropped it off."

She ducked behind the counter, shuffled in a lower drawer and popped back into view bearing a large pink envelope.

"There's no return address," Nita said, crossing over.

Curious, Elizabeth set down her fork and pried open the seal. She peeked inside then shook the contents onto the table.

What emerged had Daniel reeling back in his seat, the visual impact was so strong. At least for him.

It was a photograph of a woman standing in front of a modest house. Her arms were resting around two boys' shoulders, perhaps eight and ten years of age. All were smiling at the lens. Dark of hair and eyes, the youngest boy looked a whole lot like Jonas.

Elizabeth collected the photograph and nodded, clearly satisfied. "They're on their way to a new start."

Nita took the photo. "Fine-looking family." She offered the photo to Daniel. "Don't they look happy?"

Daniel's throat had thickened so much he wasn't sure he could squeeze any words out. He swallowed as he studied the images smiling up at him and slowly nodded.

"Yeah. They look real happy."

When the doorbell peeled through the house, Nita immediately rubbed her hands down her apron and set off. "Busier here today than the State Fair."

"She must have got her act together to have found a place to settle down in so fast," Elizabeth said, referring to that woman again as she opened the note. "It's from her sister. Says she has her eye on a good and reasonably priced car, and has an interview lined up at the diner in town tomorrow." Swiping hair behind her ear, Elizabeth read on. "But she wants to finish her education. Seems she never finished high school."

When Elizabeth lowered the letter, her gaze was distant. Daniel guessed her thoughts.

"You want to help there, too?"

She picked up the photo again and drank in the smiles, so bright and full of promise. Full of thanks and lots of tomorrows. She sighed. "This makes it all worthwhile."

Daniel sat back, certain in a way he'd never been before. Elizabeth might not have everything she wanted—freedom was a mighty big price to pay; he should know—but she was happy here with her ranch and this work. He looked around the kitchen, the old stone fireplace and, most of all, the framed photos gracing the mantel. Hell, if he'd had a real home like this, memories and such a satisfying job to do, he wouldn't leave, either.

Nita appeared at the kitchen entry, her shoulders slumped. "You have a guest, Beth."

When Chad Tremain sauntered into the room, sporting a bolo tie and steel-tipped cowboy boots, white Stetson in hand, Daniel's every muscle tensed. Then Tremain caught sight of him, too. Eyes narrowed. Mouth tightened. If he hadn't been so agitated, Daniel might have laughed. He felt as if he were about to be called out for a gunfight.

He got to his feet.

*My pleasure.*

"I haven't been able to reach you these past days," Chad said to Elizabeth while keeping his eye on Daniel. "Nita said she'd have you return my call. I was getting concerned."

"No need, Chad." Elizabeth found her feet, too. "I'm fine."

Chad's focus dropped to the plates of cake then his nose went up as if testing the air. Hospitality decreed that cake should be offered and he join them at the table. No one extended the invite.

"I believe it's my duty to inform you, in case you were unaware," Chad said, addressing Elizabeth, "that you don't have any more vacation time up your sleeve."

Daniel skirted around Elizabeth and faced Tremain square on. The man's implication was clear. He didn't want his young client being led astray by the big bad city wolf. To hell with a gunslinging showdown. How about settling this the real old-fashioned way? With fists.

"Elizabeth is well aware of her obligations," Daniel said.

Tremain looked down his nose. "Forgive me, sir, but I wasn't addressing you."

Daniel's eyebrows shot up along with his temper.

"What's your problem, Tremain? It's fine for Elizabeth to have someone speak for her, as long as it's you?"

Elizabeth stepped between the two and even held out her arms in an attempt to distance them.

"This is a waste of time," she said. "I make my own decisions."

Chad's slit gaze skipped to Elizabeth and his chest expanded on a breath. His tone, when he spoke next, was more charitable. "Of course you do, my dear."

Standing behind her, Daniel saw Elizabeth's slim shoulders roll back. "And I'll thank you not to patronize me, either, Chad."

The older man's eyes flashed before some of the red faded from his jowls and he tipped his chin a notch higher.

"Will Mr. Warren be leaving soon?" he asked. "We have important business to discuss."

When Elizabeth hesitated, unwittingly playing Tremain's control game, Daniel knew the wise choice was to take his leave. Elizabeth Milton was a gutsy, intelligent woman. She'd escape Tremain's grasp in her own way. In her own time.

He touched Elizabeth's shoulder. "I'd better go."

A mix of emotions raced over her face. Gratitude that he hadn't played out his macho card and slammed this man in the jaw. Dejection because she wanted him to stay.

"Sit down and finish your cake, Daniel." She angled back to Tremain. "Chad, from this day forward, if you have any information or thoughts to pass on, I'd appreciate if you communicated by email. I'll do the same."

Chad's face darkened. "Don't go talking rash, Elizabeth—"

"Rash?" She hacked out a humorless laugh. "I've been swallowing this unacceptable behavior for years."

"Your father—"

Her hands went up. "Don't push me, Chad. Not ever again.

If you do, I swear I'll get the best lawyer in Texas to find a loophole in that will, and by the time we've dragged you and your company through the legal mill, I'll be thirty, you'll have lost a bucket load and you *still* won't control me."

Daniel snapped shut his dropped jaw. He'd like to think he had something to do with her giving it to Tremain smack between the eyes, but that slam dunk was all Elizabeth. She'd had enough of manipulation, both before and beyond the grave.

His chest pumping in and out, Tremain opened his mouth to protest. But then his wild gaze seemed to quiet. His voice was raw when he spoke.

"I only wanted to look out for you."

After an uncertain moment, she stepped forward and laid a neutral hand on his jacketed arm. "It's time to let go."

Tremain took a couple of breaths then smiled weakly at the woman with whom he was clearly in love.

"If you need anything…"

"I'll know where you are," she said not unkindly.

Tremain turned to leave but stopped long enough to pin Daniel with a glare. "If you don't look after her, you'll have me to answer to."

As the older man strode out, Daniel mulled over his parting words. Certainly he'd taken Elizabeth away for a couple of days. They'd made love. Many times. But he had no intention of making an honest woman of her and proposing, if that's what Tremain had meant.

But the way Elizabeth was looking at him now, from beneath lowered lashes, his skin began to prickle and itch. He thought of life day in and day out on a ranch, thought of that family she'd helped, then he remembered how crap his own upbringing had been.

Years ago he'd made a vow to stay single. Not get involved. Right now he was near drowning in expectation.

He cleared his throat, looked around. Nita had made herself scarce.

"He won't bother you again," he said.

Tremain might be a determined type, but he wasn't a brute, and he wasn't stupid. Now that he knew there was no chance with Elizabeth, he'd accept reality and move on.

"I think Chad believes there's more to our relationship than there is," she said.

"I think you're right."

She let slip a short laugh. "Sounded like he actually thought you might decide to give up New York and move down here."

Her words said she didn't care but her eyes told him that was a lie. His chest closed around a great ugly knot that he knew wouldn't go away until he spoke up. They'd danced around this for too long. He needed to clear the air. Get everything out in the open, for her sake much more than his.

"If the members like my design, I'll be down this way a lot these next six months. If that happens I'd like to see you again."

A big smile lit her eyes. "I'd like that, too."

He took her hands in his. "But, Elizabeth, I have to tell you…I'm not after anything permanent. Not now. Not ever."

Her head went back and a sheet of gray seemed to drop over her face. But then she gathered herself enough for a tight smile to curve the corners of her mouth.

"Why, I don't recall asking for your hand, Mr. Warren."

He blinked at her tone. Was she teasing?

"I simply thought it was better to be honest up front," he explained.

"I agree."

"Then you're okay with it?"

"Okay with it?" Her attention dropped to the floor as she thought. When their eyes met again, her expression was devoid of emotion, except a glint of derision in her darkened eyes. "It doesn't matter what I want, does it?"

He slid his hands into his back jeans pockets. "You're making it sound as if this is some kind of surprise. As if you don't know me at all."

"I know you had a bad time growing up, being shunted between parents who put their own agendas before their children's needs. I know you lost your little brother and the pain's still as fresh as if it had happened yesterday. And I'm pretty darn sure you've never faced any of the hurt. That you'll keep dodging and running until you drop."

With every word, his pulse jumped higher and his jaw clenched tighter. She was right, of course. But it was his life, and insight didn't change the facts.

"I am what I am, Elizabeth."

"And you sure are something." Her slim nostrils flared as her shoulders crept up. "But if it's all the same with you, I'll decline on your invitation of 'maybe,' 'whenever.'"

"You don't want to see me if I get the job?"

*You want commitment? Maybe a big diamond ring?*

"You're not the only one who gets to draw up the terms," she said, and he rubbed the back of his neck. "You hadn't thought of it that way before, had you?"

His voice dropped. "I don't want to have an argument."

"No, you want to walk out and tell yourself you'd saved me a lot of pain. And guess what?" Her eyes edged with moisture. "You're probably right."

Her cheeks were flushed now and he felt his own temperature inching toward the red zone. "I knew I shouldn't have come in," he muttered at the doorway.

She crossed her arms at the same time her throat bobbed on a deep swallow.

"I'm not sorry we went away together. But, frankly, I

take offence at being slotted into a schedule when and if an opening pops up. Guess I'm old-fashioned that way."

A million thoughts raced through his mind. Not a one was appropriate to voice aloud. He exhaled. "I suppose there's nothing left to say except, I might see you around."

"I'll be here."

But when he turned to leave, she held him back.

"Daniel, wait."

He spun back. She looked so beautiful, standing in a simple yellow dress, her hair mussed after this morning's swim, skin glowing from days spent splashing and swimming and kissing. His gaze dropped to her lips. Plump. Moist.

He held back a groan.

Hell, if she wanted to reconsider, how could he say no?

Her arms unraveling, she took two steps toward him. A hint of a smile touched the corners of her lips. He was about to save her the suffering, close the distance separating them and kiss her—*show* her—he was sorry they'd argued.

But then she rubbed her palms down the sides of her skirt, lifted her chin, and said, "Good luck with that design. I'll let you see yourself out."

# Thirteen

Daniel flew back to New York that afternoon. As he'd told Elizabeth, he'd wanted to speak with Rand about the final drawings for the club and, given he had nothing keeping him in Royal at this time—nothing at all—why waste time there when he could speak to his assistant in person?

As he strode, unannounced, into his office the next morning, freshly shaven and ready to roll his sleeves up, Daniel told himself how good it was to be back. Millicent, Warren Architects' superefficient silver-haired receptionist, greeted him with a broad, denture-filled smile. Blair, his personal assistant, pushed back her chair and gaped as he breezed by and bade her good-morning. He strode into his massive, sparsely furnished office that provided a magical view of the Chrysler Building—one of the finest in the city—and let out a satisfied sigh.

The spat with Elizabeth hadn't been pleasant. He wished they'd parted on better terms. But there was no use dwelling on it. Nothing could be done about it. He was right to have left and now that he was home where he belonged, he'd stay away. No question.

Daniel settled in his high-backed leather chair, steepled his fingers under his chin and studied the panorama, courtesy of a wall of floor-to-ceiling windows. The smell of doughnuts and coffee, of hard work and success…

Knuckles rapping on wood had Daniel snapping forward in his seat. Rand had cracked open his office door.

"Heard you were in. You ready to be bombarded?"

Daniel slapped his palms on his glass-plated desk. "Fire away."

They crossed to one of the drafting tables and Rand rolled out a drawing. Daniel slipped on his glasses and scanned the details at the same time Rand gave a summary of how he'd incorporated his boss's ideas.

After half an hour of discussing matters like budget, safety regulations and material availability, Daniel removed his glasses and patted his friend on the back.

"Well done."

"I'll get to work on the model. When do we head back down? The Cattleman's Club Grand Poobahs get together next week to have a look, right?"

"Why don't we just transfer images to 3-D software? There's no need for you guys to join me for the presentation this time." A quick in and out was what was needed.

Rand leaned back against the table. "You plan to spend more time with your lady friend?"

"Not this trip." Daniel rolled up the drawing and admitted, "Not anytime in the future, actually."

Rand frowned. "You two had a falling-out?"

"More of a *time to move on* scenario."

Daniel crossed to his desk, leaving Rand to shake his head. "Goes to show. I've seen you with women before but, from the little I saw, I honestly thought you and Elizabeth Milton looked right."

Without diverting his attention from the papers he'd dragged out, Daniel issued a thin smile. "Goes to show."

Rand wandered over. "I thought you mentioned you two were going away for a couple of days."

Daniel kept his head down. "Yep. Did that."

Rand swung a hip over the corner of the desk. After a few moments, Daniel looked up.

"What?"

"You've fallen for her, haven't you?"

Appalled, Daniel pushed the papers away. "I have not."

Rand grinned. "Have to."

Growling, Daniel rolled back his chair and strode to his view of the Chrysler. His inspiration. Since he'd decided to make architecture his life, he'd dreamed of imagining a building that would have that much impact. Dignity, durability.

Daniel blew out a weary breath.

But when it came down to it, any building was only so much brick and mortar.

"Even if I *had* fallen for her," Daniel began, still peering out over Manhattan, "there's no future."

"You're afraid of committing?"

"Sure." He shrugged. "There's that. But we come from different worlds. Or rather we've chosen different worlds. She won't give up hers and I sure as hell won't be giving up mine."

Although he understood Elizabeth's situation, she'd been *given* her lifestyle. On the other hand, after he'd turned his back on his parents' bribes, he'd slogged it out and had done it on his own. He regretted not a day. More importantly, he intended to keep everything he'd earned. New York City was more than his home. It held his soul. Like Milton Ranch held Elizabeth's.

He glanced over. Rand was trying to rub away his grin.

"Did I say something funny?"

Rand showed an index finger and thumb a smidgen apart. "Maybe a tad."

Daniel strode back. "This had better be good."

"You sound like a kid in a sandbox. *I'm not giving up my ball,*" he said in a singsongy tone, "*if she doesn't give up hers.*"

Rand was a friend. A good one. He was someone Daniel listened to. But in this situation Rand was wrong.

"This isn't a game."

"That's not for me to say." Rand's expression sobered. "And if you two can't compromise then it is best you each take your ball and go home."

"Okay." Daniel threw up his hands. "Enough with the home and the balls and me not being mature enough to handle this."

"So, what do you plan to do about it?"

"Nothing."

Rand deadpanned. "Nothing."

"If Elizabeth and I were together, if I were to, you know—"

"Propose?"

"Yeah." He scratched behind his ear. "That. Even if we could work out the distance situation, she'd want a family." He thought of the commitment she'd made for her dead parents. About the money she handed over to help mothers and children in need. "Family's huge with her."

As he sat back behind his desk, heavily this time, an image of Jonas flashed in his mind. Daniel winced. *It really was all too hard. Too late.*

"Looks like you've got a lot to think over," Rand said.

Daniel scowled. "I was done thinking until you walked in."

His assistant winked and added, "You're welcome," before

he shut the door behind him, leaving Daniel to close his eyes and try to see past the shell he'd built around himself.

After a few minutes, his focus dropped to his bottom drawer and his heart began to hammer at the same time beads of sweat broke out across the back of his neck. Gaze still on that drawer, he scrubbed his jaw, his damp nape. Another few beats and he bent and jerked open the drawer before he could chicken out and change his mind.

His hand shook slightly as fingers dug beneath piles of rarely perused documents and came in contact with something smooth, cool and flat that hadn't seen the light of day in a decade.

Daniel brought the photograph higher and forced himself to absorb the image that sent bittersweet emotion rising in his chest to his throat.

Two boys smiled up at him, one a head taller than the other, their arms slung around the other's shoulders. Daniel looked at the younger boy…his white smile, dark hair, his innocent air, a splash of blue paint on his tee.

Daniel's throat convulsed and he swallowed.

Not a day went by that he didn't miss his little brother. Not a day when he didn't try to block the hurt that waited for moments just like this to leap up and tackle him until he didn't want to get up and face that reality again.

He set the photo on the desk, placed a palm over the image, closed his eyes and prayed that his brother could somehow… *feel* him. If he ever had a son of his own, would he, Daniel Warren, look like Jonas? Would he be a good father? A good husband?

Was there any chance of him and Elizabeth making it to the next step, and the next? What if they did the "marriage and family" thing and failed…failed badly? He wasn't frightened of much, but, as God was his witness, that possibility scared the life out of him. Maybe he was a coward, maybe he was running, but at least he didn't have to explain himself to anyone.

Elizabeth was *not* counting down the days.

She knew the Cattleman's Club members were meeting this afternoon to view Daniel's design, but only because Abigail hadn't quit reminding her this past week since she'd returned from that magical island...from her all too short romantic escape. For a long time afterward, all she'd been able to think about was how she had wanted to visit there with Daniel again.

Not happening, Elizabeth reminded herself as she gave Ame's neck an extra brisk brush. She was home, holding it together, and that was that.

On a positive note, she'd finally sorted out her position with Chad, and if he was hurt or angry with her for truly standing up for herself, he'd simply have to get used to it. She'd also been in touch with the shelter. Feeling restless, she'd thought there must be something more she could do to help her community's families in need. Summer Franklin, the director at the Helping Hands Shelter, had been beside herself with gratitude and ideas.

And then there was Daniel.

For the thousandth time, a vision of him laughing and chasing her in the sea bubbled up in her mind. When an area beneath her ribs panged, Elizabeth set her cheek against Ame's warm neck and, staring blindly at the stall door, allowed herself a moment to reflect. To feel.

She'd been sorry to see him go. Actually the emotion was more like devastated. When he'd walked out that day, burning tears had been horrifyingly close to falling. After having her say, which she stood by still, she'd been so near weakening, making a damn fool of herself and begging him not to go.

But the more time that went by, Elizabeth thought as she went to find an apple for Ame, the stronger she felt about agreeing not to see her charming architect again. They'd had fun together—incredible, wonderful times. That didn't mean, given their circumstances, that would continue. Daniel would not abide traipsing back and forth between North and South as he'd been forced to do when he was a child. He didn't want to live outside Manhattan and she was committed to the Lone Star State.

As Ame chomped into the fruit she held out for him, Elizabeth set her jaw. A year from now, she could be back into study, have visited Australia. Who knows? Perhaps she'd have even found a new love interest. Although she couldn't see anyone measuring up to Daniel.

Her heart dropped.

For the life of her, she couldn't envisage being with anyone again.

Ricquo stuck his head in the stall. "Sorry to interrupt. Mr. Tremain is here to see you."

Elizabeth groaned. She was tempted to take the coward's way out, shake a quieting finger at Ricquo and mime, *Tell him I'm not here*. But she was interested to know why Chad had come. If he thought her threat of legal action had been an empty one, he was mistaken. She could take a lot, just don't rub it in.

Chad appeared outside the stall. In jeans and chambray button-down, he looked ready to jump into a saddle. He sent over a warm smile.

"No need to panic. I'm not here on business. It's a personal matter I've come to see you about."

She edged forward. "Is something wrong?"

"I thought you might want a lift into town. You know the Cattleman members are meeting today. Don't you want to be there to congratulate Abigail if that new clubhouse design gets the thumbs-up?"

Touched—knowing he was sincere—Elizabeth picked up the brush again.

"That is kind of you. But I told Abigail we'd meet for a drink afterward."

"You don't want to see Daniel Warren before he leaves again? I have it on good authority he'll only be here for the length of the meeting. If the design goes through he's putting on a project manager to oversee everything he'd have been involved with during construction."

Her midsection twisted until she bit her lip to distract herself from the pain. So he didn't even want to spend work-related time here. He wanted to avoid her that much. She gave Ame another swift brush, and another. Well, that was fine by her.

But then her gaze met Chad's again and she frowned.

"Why are you telling me this?"

He gave a hapless shrug. "I want to see you happy. Always have."

The look on his face made her chest squeeze. "I thank you for that. But my happiness doesn't lie in that direction." She admitted, "Daniel and I had a disagreement."

"I heard. Not too many secrets get kept in Royal." He reached into his suede jacket's breast pocket and withdrew an envelope. "This is for you."

She stopped brushing and came forward when he set it on the stall door ledge.

"What's this?"

"Something," he said, "that could make all the difference."

Back in Royal thirty minutes, Daniel stood up at the back of the Cattleman's Club meeting room, waiting for his cue.

It felt strange being in this town again. Stranger knowing

he'd be here for only an hour or so. Elizabeth Milton was only a short drive away and he'd made up his mind he would not give in to the temptation to go to her, to see her again. He'd discussed it with Rand that day. He'd been pulled every which way since. But when all the smoke blew away, he was left with the same reality.

No matter how much they enjoyed each other's company, how well suited they might be in so many ways, the obstacles separating them were simply too great to surmount. He was not and never would be into long-distance relationships. And she had a ranch to keep.

Shaking himself, Daniel pricked his ears. Abigail was addressing the room, which was filled with low-toned murmurings and curious gazes.

"You all know my friend and leading New York architect, Daniel Warren," Abigail began. "Daniel agreed to come down today to show us his new design." Rumblings went up. So did Abigail's hands. "Some of you aren't sold on the idea of a new headquarters. Some of you aren't happy with the recent changes to membership, which allow me to address you today." She spoke over their elevated voices. "But I'll ask you to remember the club's creed and today put your hospitality and goodwill before misgivings."

Abigail looked around and when she was satisfied the mob would play nice, she tossed back her long red hair, stepped aside and waved her guest up to the head of the table.

"Gentlemen, Daniel Warren."

A reasonable amount of applause filtered through the room. Daniel smiled and bowed his head and told himself he'd had tougher audiences. But not much.

He ran a finger and thumb down his tie and began.

"In the short time I've known Royal," he said, "I've come to appreciate a little of what this community, and particularly this club, holds dear. Great pride built on great challenges has helped build these walls. I understand those who aren't ready to cheer on what they might see as the destruction of a symbol of those virtues."

He noted the few grunts of assent, even approval, took a breath and went on.

"I hope what I show you today will not only prompt you to remember the stoic roots from which this club has flourished, but also inspire you to glimpse a future that builds upon what's already remarkable and celebrated here."

Daniel nodded to Abigail. When the lights dimmed, he hit a button on his laptop keyboard and a three-dimensional lifelike image faded up on the giant portable screen behind him.

"This design encompasses everything erstwhile but also welcomes the fresh and the new."

As the color image rotated from an aerial view, highlighting the rounded snaking roof that followed the lines of a steer's horn, Daniel grinned to hear several murmurs of endorsement. The image faded into interior aspects, showing the black opal areas.

"All the favorite rooms of the club have been retained…the dining room, the library, conference room, cinema, theater, and all the sport facilities. But each section of the horns will reflect upon the Texas soldier jewel legend. The story of a brave young man returning after that war, his saddlebag filled with priceless, meaning-filled gems, inspired the founders of this organization. Directed your creed. The Cattleman Club's plaque, extolling the qualities of Leadership, Justice and Peace will retain its pride of place above the entrance door."

He gave the crowd a few minutes to digest the feel of the projected images, which were accompanied by scaled drawings, and when the screen returned to exterior points of view, he spoke again.

"In keeping with the club's progression into gender integration—" he ignored the grunts "—I propose to utilize the semicircular space left by the concave angle of each horn in fitting ways. One space will house a statue of a cattleman on horseback accompanied by his cattlewoman, also in the saddle. The other side will house a playground, complete with a sitter, should any future female members wish to leave their children to exercise in the sunshine while they conduct business."

His last words were met with increasing unrest among some and interested noises from others. He gave a look Abigail's way. She sent him a wink, but in the dimmed light he wondered if she'd gone ghostly pale. She'd told him to run with any innovative ideas he'd had. That last was certainly a doozy.

Bradford Price, who'd kept quiet till now, stepped forward.

"With all due respect, Mr. Warren, you must be pulling our leg."

With a crooked smile and feigned look of exasperation, Price glanced around to garner support. A number of men grumbled and rallied around him. Bolstered, he spoke louder.

"The Texas Cattleman's Club has a solid, community-focused background. And I concede that with your limited knowledge, you've done a half-decent job of bringing that sentiment to the fore, Mr. Warren. Together we support our town and, in the proper circumstances, those in need beyond our borders. Leadership. Justice. Peace." Like a lawyer addressing his jury, Bradford Price strolled down the line of attentive members. "We're community-minded men. Or," he slid a suitably contrite grin Abigail's way, "should I say *people*. But, fellow members, this is not a place to babysit children. It's a place to come together and—"

Bradford's words faded at the same time his expression grew curious and an odd sound filtered into the room—an uncommon noise in these surrounds and yet, given their discussion, also perhaps a timely one. Somewhere nearby an infant was crying, the wails growing stronger and louder by the second. Puzzled members looked at one another and mutterings in the crowd became more pronounced. Daniel caught phrases like:

"The crying's coming from the outside."

"Where's the mother, for Pete's sake?"

"Can someone closer to the door see what the heck's going on?"

As the presentation slides ended, the lights came up and a man with a handlebar mustache strode out. He returned in short order.

"It's a baby, all right," the man said. "An abandoned baby in a basket set dead center on our doorstep. Looks like a note's pinned to the blanket."

Daniel was forced to step back as a wave of members washed around him and out the door. He looked for Abigail but she'd joined the exodus. As Bradford moved by, Daniel noted his suddenly pasty complexion.

Daniel had almost forgotten that overheard conversation weeks before. Now snatches of Bradford Price's tête-à-tête came echoing back. Two words, in particular.

*Baby* and *blackmail.*

How wonderful it felt to have hope! Slim as it was.

After Chad had surprised her earlier by handing over that incredible piece of information, Elizabeth jumped in her Cobra and had thought hard about breaking all land speed records to be alongside Daniel when he presented his drawings.

She'd known Daniel didn't believe in family. Given his background, in all honesty, she couldn't say she blamed him. No doubt he'd be concerned that if he were to ever get married, have a family of his own, the marriage might end in divorce. If that marriage was between Daniel and her, the likelihood of any children being shunted between states, as he had been as a child, was more than a possibility.

But maybe the document Chad had provided would change some of that thinking. She wasn't expecting Daniel to clasp his hands in thanks, fall to one knee and propose on the spot. But she wondered whether he cared enough to listen to what she had to say.

When they'd been together on that island, she'd felt herself falling. She'd hoped that after he'd left to go back to New York those feelings might fade, even a little. But the knowledge that she was in love with Daniel had only grown stronger, more insistent, until lately, she would simply lie awake at night and think of what "might have been." No matter how she tried to bury those thoughts or sweep them aside, the truth was clear.

She was in love with Daniel Warren.

And love was a powerful, stubborn thing.

Elizabeth glanced across at the passenger seat and smiled until her heart ached. The contents of that envelope might not be the answer to all of her and Daniel's problems, but at least now she felt she had a chance.

Her gaze swung back to the road in time to see the sign for the clubhouse turnoff. She put on her turning signal, but frowned when she saw what was in front of her. Had the whole town turned out to see what the members would decide regarding the proposed clubhouse design? Pickups, luxury sedans, even a couple of trucks, were lined up bumper to bumper. She wouldn't make it past this bottleneck for a good thirty minutes at least.

Daniel could be gone by then.

As she took the turn into the clubhouse road and slowed down, Elizabeth reminded herself she could telephone or, now, even fly up to see him. But that option left her feeling uneasy. Texans were known for their pride and she wasn't any different. She could show up here today on the pretext of supporting him, mention the contents of that envelope and sit back to see what happened from there. It was a gamble but no brutal thumps to her self-esteem if he smiled cordially, said he was pleased for her and goodbye. If she phoned him out of the blue or, worse, appeared on his New York City doorstep, she couldn't live with the shame if he turned her away.

Inhaling, she set her hands more firmly on the steering wheel as her car slowed to a stop. There was nothing for it but to make sure they saw each other today. No matter what.

When the screech of approaching tires had her glancing into the rearview mirror, her grip on the wheel tightened more. A bright red car barreling up behind must have been driven by the devil himself. Then Elizabeth's eyes widened and her fast-beating heart flew up the back of her throat. She had barely enough time to realize her plans for seeing Daniel today were history before the maniac's car smashed full force into the rear of hers.

Daniel had followed the rest of the crowd out to a nearby doorway. Now a wall of curious onlookers blocked his view, but the noise was unmistakable. A baby was crying, demanding attention and care. He was no expert, but it sounded like a newborn.

He risked a glance skyward. If he hadn't known better, he'd have thought someone was on his side, making a point that this place ought to dust off their agendas and acknowledge family concerns in a more hands-on way.

He'd been looking for something meaningful to incorporate into those outdoor semicircles. Seeing how connected Elizabeth was to her land, knowing how she'd helped that family and many like them—and given that Abigail, a woman, was running for presidency of the club—it had seemed timely to go that one step further, incorporating the playground and child-minding area for the future female members with kids.

Above all, he got that Royal was a caring community. The Cattleman's Club was an institution that was well-known for defending those who couldn't defend themselves. The way he figured, they'd either embrace his innovative ideas or run him out of town.

But this baby had stolen the show and rightly so.

Now, as he craned to peer over the tops of heads and between shoulders, Daniel saw how tiny he was. Cute, with lungs that wouldn't deflate, which was a sign of good health, wasn't it? He hadn't had anything to do with babies. Couldn't see now that he ever would. But somebody was responsible for the making of this one. Could it be the somebody who was loosening the Windsor knot from around his throat like it was an ever-tightening noose?

A man lifted the note from the bassinet then made a face as if he was worried the world might soon end. He handed the paper over to none other than Bradford Price.

"This here's for you," the man said. "The note *and* the baby. Says he's yours, Brad. Says time's up and you need to face up to your responsibilities."

Abigail had come to stand nearby. As Price took the note with a slightly trembling hand, then gazed disbelievingly at the baby, she braced her weight against the column at her back.

Daniel rubbed his jaw. And people thought New York was rife with scandal. But in some ways he was impressed. Clearly this man felt those critical eyes upon him, waiting for a response. A denial or a confession. But, although beads of sweat glistened on his forehead, Brad continued to stand tall, remarkably poised under pressure. Nevertheless, he had some serious back-pedaling to do if he wanted to regain the ground lost today. The spreading drone of displeasure didn't bode well for Bradford's election hopes. Even if he could prove he wasn't this abandoned baby's daddy, dirt was difficult to wash away.

"Seems your opponent might have a shaky road ahead if he wants to captain this team," he said in Abigail's ear.

Her cheeks were red. "I don't believe we'll be reconvening today's meeting anytime soon." She touched his arm. "Sorry, Daniel."

"You call me when you're ready to talk." But she looked so pale, he had to ask. "Are you okay?"

"Just wondering what's behind all this." Flipping back her mane of hair, she straightened and shouldered her way through the flock of men. "Someone needs to tend to that baby."

Stepping aside, Daniel glanced toward the parking lot and found his rental car. He'd leave Abigail a copy of his presentation to look through again, along with any other members who might be interested. It was time he checked out.

After leaving a disk on the table and collecting his laptop, Daniel made his way down the path, his thoughts back on Elizabeth…how close she was, how no good could come from him seeing her. Did she know he was in Royal today? His secretary had received a call asking when he was due. He'd thought it might've been Elizabeth. But Blair said it had been a man who had hung up before leaving his name when she'd told him her boss's visit to Royal would be a very brief one.

Someone from the club perhaps? Point was, it hadn't been Elizabeth inquiring. And if she could stay away, he'd best oblige and do the same.

Daniel was leaning into the driver's side of his rental when an almighty crash rent the air. His heart flew to his mouth as he shot bolt upright and scanned the vicinity. A lineup of cars choked the road leading to the clubhouse. Farther down toward the turnoff, a hissing smoke was rising. Seconds later the stink of burned tires filled his lungs. Daniel flinched. Whoever had taken it up the bumper would be in for a night at the local hospital. And that was if he were lucky.

Slipping back into the driver's seat—knowing authorities and assistance would be on the scene soon—Daniel started the engine and swerved carefully out onto the road. In the distance he heard a siren. Sitting tall in his seat, he noted the crowd gathering around the wrecks. He hadn't been in a car accident for over a decade. Unless he counted that ding when Elizabeth had backed into him.

She'd been sitting outside his hotel, wondering whether she ought to suck up the courage to knock on his door again. Thinking of how sheepish she'd looked that day, Daniel's blood warmed and he smiled. He'd have welcomed her intrusion. Despite the way she'd dressed him down the other day, she was still the most amazing woman he'd known. Would ever know. Such contradictions in personal strength and feminine charm; however, she did leave something to be desired when behind the wheel. He didn't want to think about her Cobra's repair bill, even for that minor damage. You didn't see too many of those around. And Elizabeth had looked like the quintessential princess....

The accident scene had come into view and Daniel's thoughts slowed to a crawl before a stinging chill enveloped his entire body. Between two others, a car was crushed. An expensive sports car.

A Cobra.

Daniel didn't shut down his engine. He was out on the road and beside the wreck before he'd taken another breath. Three policemen were on the scene. A couple of paramedics were wheeling a gurney toward an ambulance tailgate. Daniel's skin went cold from his crown to his toes. A blanket lay over the body. Her head was turned away and he couldn't get a look at the face. All he could see was a stream of blond brushed by a gentle breeze.

A lion, teeth and claws bared, leaped up inside of him. He lunged, but the nearest officer caught his arm and another joined to rustle him back. Daniel's mouth didn't want to work. It took a few seconds to push out the words.

"I know that woman."

The officer nodded, patient but firm. "It's a small town, sir. Stand back and let us look after her for you."

Daniel groaned, a harsh, desperate sound. "You don't understand."

Slanting his head, the officer looked him up and down. "You're her husband?"

Daniel swallowed against a suddenly desert-dry throat. He'd never felt more helpless. More alone.

"No," he admitted. "We're not married."

"Then you'll have to step aside."

Daniel stumbled back. It was only the fact that he'd hinder rather than help Elizabeth's chances that he let the gurney slide into the back of the ambulance without making sure he was going along for the ride. A sickening moment later, the siren blared again, taking her to...

Where was the nearest hospital?

He strode back to the officer, who was directing the squeeze of traffic. "Where are they taking her?"

"To Royal Memorial." The man's eyes held his. "If it's critical, she'll be transferred."

Daniel staggered to lean against a tree. All the precious days and hours they'd spent together bombarded his brain. How badly was she injured? Would she live?

As a narrowing black tunnel zoomed toward him, Daniel shivered as the ice in his veins began to tingle and heat. A line of perspiration erupted down his back, across his brow.

He couldn't swallow past the nausea pushing up the back of his throat.

He had to get to that hospital.

Damn it, he had to get there fast.

# Fourteen

Muffled, unfamiliar sounds filtered into Elizabeth's consciousness. Someone's voice. The beep of a machine. Squeaking of tiny wheels whirring away. Elizabeth moved her head to the side and winced as pain shot up her right side. Her neck hurt. So did her chest. And now odd smells were invading her senses.

Antiseptic?

Freshly laundered sheets.

As if her mind were swimming in molasses, her thoughts wound slowly back. Something important had happened. She just needed a moment to focus and think what…

When Elizabeth next heard voices, machines, she felt less heavy. Wasn't so aware of the pain. Although she was more aware of herself and her surroundings. Of where she must be.

Drowsy, she forced her eyes to open and took a few deep breaths.

She was lying in a bed in a private hospital suite, she guessed at Royal Memorial. And now she remembered why.

She'd been on her way to see Daniel with important news. There'd been a bottleneck leading up to the club. She'd felt impatient. Then came the squeal of brakes. After the collision, an ambulance had transported her to the hospital. A doctor checked her over and asked simple questions...her name, where she lived. He'd ordered further tests then had given her medication for the pain, something that had helped her settle and sleep.

Moaning, Elizabeth closed her eyes again.

The accident hadn't been her fault. There was nothing she could have done to prevent it. Frankly, she cared far more about another situation. She wasn't certain how much time had passed, but surely Daniel would have left Royal by now. Boarded his jet and winged it back home.

She dragged her gaze around.

Exactly how long had she been lying here?

A quiet voice.

"She's awake."

Cushions squished and then a face appeared before her. A friendly, wonderfully familiar face.

"How are you feeling, *chiquita?*"

Elizabeth moved her arms, her legs, and her head. She flinched. "My neck hurts a little."

"Do you remember what happened?"

"Most of it. It wasn't my fault."

Smiling softly, Nita ran a hand down her arm. "Whether or not the accident was your fault doesn't matter. You'll have bruises, some whiplash. Thank the Lord, nothing serious."

"How long have I been here?"

"A few hours."

Still groggy, she frowned. "I've been asleep all the time?"

"Resting. You need rest still."

"I was on my way to the clubhouse..."

"Seems you missed out on quite a show. Word's already ripped through town. Abigail's meeting was interrupted by a surprise guest."

"Who?"

"A baby, left abandoned on the clubhouse steps. A note was found. It said Bradford Price is the father."

Elizabeth's mind whirled with questions as she tried to digest the news. If Brad was the father, who was the mother? Had he known about the baby? Was the claim true or was someone out to discredit him? What did the allegation mean for the election and Abigail's plans for a new clubhouse? Where would all this leave Daniel?

Deep in thought, Elizabeth absently studied the room. Large. Clean. White. A beautiful spray of flowers sat near the window. Elizabeth's heartbeat ratcheted up and, smiling, she shimmied and tried to sit up. When her neck twinged again, she set her teeth and lowered back down.

"Those flowers...?"

"Very pretty." Nita smiled. "Very bright."

Elizabeth heard her heartbeat pounding with hope in her ears. Was Daniel still here? Perhaps he'd heard about her accident before he'd had a chance to leave?

"Who are they from?"

"I'll bring you the card."

A moment later, Elizabeth focused on the handwritten note. Her heart and hand dropped at the signature.

"They're from Chad."

"He's been here the whole time."

She stared blindly at the ceiling. "He needn't have bothered."

"You can't stop someone from caring simply because you don't care that way for them." Nita held her hand. "But remember what you told me before you sped off in your car yesterday?"

Elizabeth cast her mind back and recalled.

"I said that Chad had let me know that Daniel would only be here in Royal for a short time." Her gaze fell away. "He offered to drive me to the club so I could see him."

"Chadwick is a man who likes to be in control, a man who cares for a woman he should have known would never care for him. But that doesn't make him a bad man."

Elizabeth remembered the envelope and surrendered to a smile.

"You're right." She flipped her hand over and squeezed Nita's. "You're always right."

Nita chuckled and her glasses fell down the slope of her nose. "Glad we agree."

A nurse appeared and elevated the bed's backrest slightly. Elizabeth swallowed the pills she was offered with some water. The nurse wrote on the folder hanging off the end of the bed and, with an instruction to buzz if Elizabeth needed anything, left the other two women alone.

Nita's earlier light expression had grown solemn.

"Beth, do you feel strong enough to see a visitor? It's someone who says they want to thank you."

Elizabeth thought for a moment. "The woman from the shelter? The one who sent that photo?"

Rather than answer, Nita sent a covert glance toward the door, which was not quite closed. A set of masculine fingers were curled around the door frame. Elizabeth held her breath and blinked as her heartbeat began to gallop. Was her visitor who she guessed? Who she hoped?

Out the corner of her eye, she saw Nita give a small nod. The door fanned wider and Daniel stepped into the room.

A rush of emotion filled Elizabeth's throat, and her skin was tingling as if she'd suddenly been brought out of a deep freeze. He was more handsome than she'd even remembered. Taller. Sexier. But his eyes were the same. Green pools she wanted to drown in forever.

But when he took a step nearer and another, Elizabeth gathered herself. Daniel was a gentleman. Logic said that when he'd found out about her accident, he'd decided to delay his return to New York. That didn't mean that he'd changed his mind about them. Just because she imagined something more glittering in his eyes didn't make it so. She needed to get those thoughts out of her head.

Nita patted her arm. "I'll be outside."

With moisture blurring her vision, Elizabeth watched the older woman go. Feeling as if she couldn't quite catch her breath, she curled her toes as Daniel moved closer, stopping beside her bed. His woodsy male scent enveloped her at the same time those gorgeous eyes glittered down.

"That car of yours is going to need a whole lot more work than last time."

And then, despite the avalanche of emotions at seeing Daniel again, Elizabeth remembered the other drivers. Her hand fisted in the sheet.

"Was anyone else hurt?"

He sat down on the side of the bed. "Not seriously. Appears the guy who rammed you was busy texting. He almost missed the turnoff and tried to correct the oversteer while going too damn fast. His car's a write-off."

"Cars can be replaced."

His big, warm hand found hers. "Precisely what I've been telling myself."

The contact of his skin on hers sent a flurry of bright-tipped sparks hurtling through her system. Before she'd thought she'd almost sighed and brought her other hand over to double the effect. Whenever he'd touch her, she'd felt as if nothing else mattered. Just for a few minutes, she would have let herself believe that again.

"When do you have to be back in New York?" she made herself ask.

"I was expected hours ago."

Talk about having the remains of a fantasy demolished in one fell swoop. She'd been wondering if, or when, she might mention the document Chad had given her. Now she was glad she hadn't opened her big, stupid mouth. He was here but clearly he wanted to get back home as soon as possible. Boil that all down and...

He didn't love her.

Well, of course he didn't.

What possible difference could her bit of news make?

Her throat clogged with disappointment, she slipped her hand from beneath his.

He held her gaze for a long moment before he drew away and moved toward a window. Did he have his jet ready and waiting to take him away as soon as he could assure himself his former lover was well on the mend?

"I'm not happy you had that accident," he said, gazing out over the hospital grounds. "But I am glad we've had a chance to see each other again."

Elizabeth's lips tightened. Well, he'd seen her now. He could walk away guilt-free. In fact, she wished he'd go. Leave her be and go now.

But when he slowly turned to face her, she melted in a new way that left her aching and despising herself. The image his silhouette cut against the incoming filtered light was entirely masculine, überpowerful. She'd spent so many hours pressed up against him, listening to his murmurings as they made love every chance they got. Feeling as though life couldn't get any better.

She groaned at herself and, despite the fading pain in her

neck, thanks to those pills, she turned away. If she could cut out her heart and rid herself of him that way, she would gladly take a knife and do it.

"If you need to be on your way," she said, knowing her voice sounded thick, "please don't let me keep you."

She could hear him breathe. She imagined his broad chest expanding then noted his footfall as he crossed back over.

"Are you comfortable?" he asked after an agonizing time.

She thought about it then exhaled. If he was staying a few minutes, she might as well be comfortable.

"I wouldn't mind sitting up a little more," she admitted.

"Let me know if it hurts and I'll stop."

She wanted to say straight out, *Yes, it hurts*. Please stop. Please go away. But then he found the remote, pressed a button and the mattress behind her back began to tilt up.

"That's fine, thank you," she said when she was sitting at what she deemed to be a respectable angle.

His gaze down, he paced around her bed one way then back again.

"Are you trying to make me dizzy?"

He rolled back one shoulder and let his gaze mesh with hers.

"Elizabeth, I've been thinking these past twenty-four hours. Thinking a lot. About my past. My parents. Most of all, I've thinking about you."

Whether she was going to be okay? She wasn't a big fan of pity.

"Daniel, I truly don't think there's any reason to be concerned—"

"Not about the accident," he cut in, then tempered the interruption with, "Or not solely."

She wiggled up higher on the pillows. She told herself to keep things in perspective, but now she was curious.

"Go on."

"My father's mansion is a building passed down for generations," he told her. "I wanted nothing to do with its somber portraits and musty parlors. Most of all I wanted nothing to do with the family plots arranged on an adjoining piece of land."

He shut his eyes, rubbed a point between his eyebrows and Elizabeth's heart went out to him. Family plots. A cemetery. That's where his brother must be buried.

"I understand," she told him, her tone softer. "If I were you I wouldn't want anything to do with it, either. Except…"

"You're wondering if I've ever gone back to see my brother's grave. The answer's no. And I need to. After seeing you being driven away in an ambulance, after sitting out there hour after endless hour, I see that now very clearly."

Nodding to himself, he paced around the bed a second time but then pulled up abruptly as if the right words had popped into his head.

"You were right about me running away. I didn't want to face all those memories that made me so damn mad. Made me feel so helpless."

The last word was said with such sadness, if she'd been able, Elizabeth would have wound her arms around him and whispered that was a long time ago.

Instead, she let her compassion take a less intimate road and reminded him, "You said yourself, you're an adult now."

He set his hands on his hips, grunted then came to sit once again on the bed at her side.

"I might be an adult but I'm not sure I acted with much maturity once I was older. I pretty much ran away to a place where I didn't have to face the things grown-ups sometimes need to."

"Like when someone passes away?" she offered quietly.

"I've been so tied up in keeping ahead of the game, never wanting to look over my shoulder, I've missed out on what I had left. Worse, I thought I'd be happy keeping my head in the clouds."

An urgent look came to his face and he sat closer.

"Do you know," he said, "I don't even own my apartment in Manhattan? Crazy, huh? The places I live in get bigger and better, and I tell myself New York's my home. Yet I keep shifting, certain I'll find that one perfect place to put out the welcome mat for good." His eyebrows knitted. "The closest I've ever felt to home is that time we spent on our island."

Elizabeth was sitting, stunned, trying to take in this glut of information. Daniel didn't own his own apartment? He'd felt most at home with her?

"What I'm trying to say, Elizabeth, is that it's not walls and a roof that make a home. It's the person—or people—you're with."

Her throat closed off at the same time a single hot tear trailed from the corner of her eye. More tears were banked up, threatening to spill.

Pressing her lips together, hoping to contain some of the emotion, she nodded. "I agree."

His fingers wrapped around her upper arm and he leaned in close, so near she could see the darker flecks of jade in his eyes, see the sincerity and need that begged for her to listen.

"I have a lot of friends up North. A lot of business connections, acquaintances. Hell, I have fifteen years of history in New York. I love Broadway and Central Park. I love Chinatown and the restaurants and knowing I live in the most awesome city in the world. But, my God, I love you more." His lips grazed hers. "Infinitely and forever more."

Silent tears were spilling down her cheeks. She'd dreamed of such a moment but her imagination had never come close to the depth of Daniel's admission now.

He loved her?

She flung her arms around him.

*He loves me!*

When the receding pain in her neck bit, she swallowed a yelp and eased back against the pillows.

"I have something to tell you, too." She felt the bubbles of excitement rising up and exploding inside of her.

He held up a palm. "Please, Elizabeth. Let me finish." He brought his crooked knee up on the bed and leaned back toward her. "I'll leave New York—"

"You'd leave your company?"

"I'd leave Rand in charge of that office. I can start a branch up down here. No reason why it can't work. I always wanted offices all over the world. This can be my start."

"All over the world—"

"But, don't worry," he cut in. "I won't go trekking around without you. You have two months a year." He kissed her temple. "We can do a lot in two months."

"Is this what I think it is?"

He brought her hand to his scratchy chin and looked solemnly into her eyes.

"I want to marry you. I want you to be my wife. For better or worse. In sickness, in health, in everything life has to throw our way. I'll be there for the long haul and I promise to always put your needs, and the needs of our family first. If we both want to make it work, I know we won't fail."

Those tears backed up again, choking. Liberating. "You'd give up your life for me?"

"I want to *start* my life with you."

She let it sink in then blew out a long, giddy breath. She wanted to bring him close, kiss him hard, tell him that she loved him, too. But she couldn't.

Not yet.

"Before I answer, there's something you should know."

His gaze narrowed for a heartbeat as if he expected the

worst. But then he pressed his lips to the inside of her wrist and held her hand all the tighter.

"Shoot."

"Chad came to visit me yesterday."

She saw it was a struggle for him to keep a neutral face. "And?"

"And it seems I wasn't talking out my ear when I mentioned finding a loophole to the will if I had to."

A smile kicked up one corner of his mouth. "Tell me more."

"Not only did he offer to drive me to the club to support you, he also gave me a document that had been drawn up by my parents in addition to their will. The caveat on my time spent away from the ranch was supposed to be up until my thirtieth birthday. That is, unless Chad was convinced it was in my best interest to waive that clause."

Looking bewildered, Daniel shook his head.

"Sorry. I just had a disturbing image of Tremain dressed as a fairy godmother."

She laughed. "He said when he knew I truly wanted to keep the ranch but was suffering so badly because of my restrictions he decided to act on behalf of my parents."

"Do you think you have your mother to thank for that document?"

She considered it. "I'd like to believe my parents worked it out together."

He bundled her up in his arms. "Together sounds good."

She tried but couldn't help flinching at the bite in her neck. He laid her back down quickly but gently.

"I'd love to sweep you up, carry you away, but I'm betting the doc will want to keep you in overnight for observation."

"That won't stop me."

His eyebrows pinched over an amused smile. "Stop you from what?"

"From ravaging you. I take it you do want to be ravaged."

"That depends."

She coughed out a laugh. "On what?"

"You haven't given me your answer yet."

He leaned in and, as his mouth covered hers, Elizabeth fell headlong into that warm, wonderful bliss Daniel never failed to build up inside of her. Her hands reached to comb through his hair while her body arced toward his heat, his indisputable love.

This was the best day of her life.

When he slowly broke the kiss, he let out a satisfied breath and set his forehead to hers.

"Now, you can give me your answer. No answer's wrong, as long as it's yes."

She laughed again. "In that case, it's a definite *yes*."

With his trademark sexy grin, he moved to kiss her again but then pulled back. "Almost forgot. I have something for you."

He eased away and, a moment later, bent to collect something sitting outside the door. When she realized what he was bringing back, she was puzzled.

"You brought me a painting?"

"I remembered how much you wanted a *Water Lilies*," he said, keeping the back of the painting facing her.

Her thoughts were racing. "You bought me a Monet?"

A ten-by-twelve inch?

He rotated the painting. Her heart skipped a beat then a laugh of surprise and thanks escaped. She could tell it was a genuine attempt, but it had obviously been created by an amateur. And an untalented one at that.

"Daniel, did *you* paint that picture?"

"I got some materials in and dabbled while you were sleeping. Now I realize I should've used that time finding the perfect ring."

Her heart bursting with passion and love, she signaled for

him to come nearer then, gripping his shirt, she tugged him close.

"I don't care about diamonds," she said into his eyes.

"Not even an eternity ring? I believe they're required when the first child is born."

Just like that, her eyes filled again, this time until happy tears sped down her cheeks. Her voice came out a raspy, thankful squeak.

"You want to have children?"

"At least a couple. Maybe three or four." A shadow briefly crossed his eyes. "And I want them to meet their grandparents. We should do this the right way. Everyone included. Nobody feeling they don't matter."

A salty tear curled into the side of her mouth, then coursed down around her chin.

"I love you, Daniël. More than I even knew."

He wiped away her next tear. "We'll grow old together." He pretended to frown. "Although I'll have a head start there."

"When we're octogenarians with great-grandchildren rolling us around in our wheelchairs, do you think that'll matter?"

"This, my darling, is what matters."

When he kissed her again, Elizabeth wanted to sigh and, with her heartfelt embrace, told him she agreed. Being together, and seizing and building on their magical newfound love, was more important than anything.

* * * * *

# COMING NEXT MONTH

### Available November 8, 2011

**#2119 WANTED BY HER LOST LOVE**
Maya Banks
*Pregnancy & Passion*

**#2120 TEMPTATION**
Brenda Jackson
*Texas Cattleman's Club: The Showdown*

**#2121 NOTHING SHORT OF PERFECT**
Day Leclaire
*Billionaires and Babies*

**#2122 RECLAIMING HIS PREGNANT WIDOW**
Tessa Radley

**#2123 IMPROPERLY WED**
Anna DePalo

**#2124 THE PRICE OF HONOR**
Emilie Rose

---

You can find more information on upcoming
Harlequin® titles, free excerpts and more at
**www.HarlequinInsideRomance.com.**

---

HDCNM1011

# REQUEST YOUR FREE BOOKS!
## 2 FREE NOVELS PLUS 2 FREE GIFTS!

## ALWAYS POWERFUL, PASSIONATE AND PROVOCATIVE

**YES!** Please send me 2 FREE Harlequin Desire® novels and my 2 FREE gifts (gifts are worth about $10). After receiving them, if I don't wish to receive any more books, I can return the shipping statement marked "cancel." If I don't cancel, I will receive 6 brand-new novels every month and be billed just $4.30 per book in the U.S. or $4.99 per book in Canada. That's a saving of at least 14% off the cover price! It's quite a bargain! Shipping and handling is just 50¢ per book in the U.S. and 75¢ per book in Canada.* I understand that accepting the 2 free books and gifts places me under no obligation to buy anything. I can always return a shipment and cancel at any time. Even if I never buy another book, the two free books and gifts are mine to keep forever.

225/326 HDN FEF3

Name _____ (PLEASE PRINT) _____

Address _____ Apt. #

City _____ State/Prov. _____ Zip/Postal Code

Signature (if under 18, a parent or guardian must sign)

### Mail to the **Reader Service:**
**IN U.S.A.:** P.O. Box 1867, Buffalo, NY 14240-1867
**IN CANADA:** P.O. Box 609, Fort Erie, Ontario L2A 5X3

Not valid for current subscribers to Harlequin Desire books.

**Want to try two free books from another line?**
**Call 1-800-873-8635 or visit www.ReaderService.com.**

\* Terms and prices subject to change without notice. Prices do not include applicable taxes. Sales tax applicable in N.Y. Canadian residents will be charged applicable taxes. Offer not valid in Quebec. This offer is limited to one order per household. All orders subject to credit approval. Credit or debit balances in a customer's account(s) may be offset by any other outstanding balance owed by or to the customer. Please allow 4 to 6 weeks for delivery. Offer available while quantities last.

**Your Privacy**—The Reader Service is committed to protecting your privacy. Our Privacy Policy is available online at www.ReaderService.com or upon request from the Reader Service.

We make a portion of our mailing list available to reputable third parties that offer products we believe may interest you. If you prefer that we not exchange your name with third parties, or if you wish to clarify or modify your communication preferences, please visit us at www.ReaderService.com/consumerschoice or write to us at Reader Service Preference Service, P.O. Box 9062, Buffalo, NY 14269. Include your complete name and address.

HDES11B

*Harlequin® Special Edition® is thrilled to present a new installment in* USA TODAY *bestselling author RaeAnne Thayne's reader-favorite miniseries,* THE COWBOYS OF COLD CREEK.

*Join the excitement as we meet the Bowmans—four siblings who lost their parents but keep family ties alive in Pine Gulch. First up is Trace. Only two things get under this rugged lawman's skin: beautiful women and secrets. And in Rebecca Parsons, he finds both!*

*Read on for a sneak peek of*
*CHRISTMAS IN COLD CREEK.*
*Available November 2011 from Harlequin® Special Edition®.*

On impulse, he unfolded himself from the bar stool. "Need a hand?"

"Thank you! I…" She lifted her gaze from the floor to his jeans and then raised her eyes. When she identified him her hazel eyes turned from grateful to unfriendly and cold, as if he'd somehow thrown the broken glasses at her head.

He also thought he saw a glimmer of panic in those interesting depths, which instantly stirred his curiosity like cream swirling through coffee.

"I've got it, Officer. Thank you." Her voice was several degrees colder than the whirl of sleet outside the windows.

Despite her protests, he knelt down beside her and began to pick up shards of broken glass. "No problem. Those trays can be slippery."

This close, he picked up the scent of her, something fresh and flowery that made him think of a mountain meadow on a July afternoon. She had a soft, lush mouth and for one brief, insane moment, he wanted to push aside that stray lock of hair slipping from her ponytail and taste her. Apparently he needed to spend a lot less time working and a great deal *more* time recreating with the opposite sex if he could have sudden random fantasies about a woman he wasn't even inclined to like, pretty or not.

"I'm Trace Bowman. You must be new in town."

She didn't answer immediately and he could almost see the wheels turning in her head. Why the hesitancy? And why that little hint of unease he could see clouding the edge of her gaze? His presence was obviously making her uncomfortable and Trace couldn't help wondering why.

"Yes. We've been here a few weeks."

"Well, I'm just up the road about four lots, in the white house with the cedar shake roof, if you or your daughter need anything." He smiled at her as he picked up the last shard of glass and set it on her tray.

Definitely a story there, he thought as she hurried away. He just might need to dig a little into her background to find out why someone with fine clothes and nice jewelry, and who so obviously didn't have experience as a waitress, would be here slinging hash at The Gulch. Was she running away from someone? A bad marriage?

So...Rebecca Parsons. Not Becky. An intriguing woman. It had been a long time since one of those had crossed his path here in Pine Gulch.

*Trace won't rest until he finds out Rebecca's secret, but will he still have that same attraction to her once he does? Find out in CHRISTMAS IN COLD CREEK. Available November 2011 from Harlequin® Special Edition®.*

**Harlequin** *Desire*

ALWAYS POWERFUL, PASSIONATE AND PROVOCATIVE.

*NEW YORK TIMES* AND *USA TODAY*
BESTSELLING AUTHOR

# BRENDA JACKSON

**PRESENTS A BRAND-NEW TALE
OF SEDUCTION**

## TEMPTATION

Millionaire security expert and rancher Zeke Travers
always separates emotion from work. Until a case
leads him to Sheila Hopkins—and the immediate,
scorching heat that leaped between them. Suddenly,
Zeke is tempted to break the rules. And it's only a
matter of time before he gives in....

*Available November wherever books are sold.*

HD73133

brings you

*USA TODAY* Bestselling Author

## Penny Jordan

Part of the new miniseries

### RUSSIAN RIVALS

*Demidov vs. Androvonov—let the most
merciless of men win...*

**Kiryl Androvonov**

The Russian oligarch has one rival: billionaire
Vasilii Demidov. Luckily, Vasilii has an Achilles' heel—his
younger, overprotected, beautiful half sister, Alena...

**Vasilii Demidov**

After losing his sister to his bitter rival, Vasilii is far too
cynical to ever trust a woman, not even his secretary Laura.
Never did she expect to be at the ruthless Russian's mercy....

*The rivalry begins in...*

THE MOST COVETED PRIZE—November
THE POWER OF VASILII—December

**Available wherever
Harlequin Presents® books are sold.**

# ROMANTIC
## SUSPENSE

# CARLA CASSIDY
## *Cowboy's Triplet Trouble*

Jake Johnson, the eldest of his triplet brothers, is stunned
when Grace Sinclair turns up on his family's ranch declaring
Jake's younger and irresponsible brother as the father of her
triplets. When Grace's life is threatened, Jake finds himself
fighting a powerful attraction and a need to protect. But as
the threats hit closer to home, Jake begins to wonder
if someone on the ranch is out to kill Grace....

**A brand-new Top Secret Deliveries story!**

*Available in November wherever books are sold!*

www.Harlequin.com

HRS27751